C000212452

The Permanent Way

MARIE CROSS

Wrate's Publishing

First published in 2023 by Wrate's Publishing

ISBN 978-1-7396165-8-8

Copyright © 2023 by Marie Cross

Edited and typeset by Wrate's Editing Services

www.wrateseditingservices.co.uk

Cover design by Rachel Middleton

Cover drawing taken from *The Illustrated Guide to the South Eastern Railway* by George Measom by kind permission of Countryside Books, Newbury, Berkshire: info@countrysidebooks.co.uk

A CIP catalogue record for this book is available from the British Library.

This book is dedicated to my father, William Martin, who worked on the railway all his life.

Preface

My reasons for writing this book are threefold; I like writing (this is my fifth novel), I live in Tonbridge and I am a railwayman's daughter!

I have extensively researched the background for this story, but I have had to assume many aspects. Mr Hubber was a real sub contractor, but it is extremely unlikely he had such a person as a runner. However, I wanted to give a flavour of the upheaval that must have transpired with the building of England's permanent way: not only that, but the difference it made to people's lives when completed.

Part One

Chapter One

YANK LEFT the Barleycorn behind him and strode out into the black night air. The sounds of his fellow workers singing and shouting in the beer house faded as he rounded the bend. Their own night, he knew, had hardly started; they would no doubt be drinking and carousing for some while yet, before time was called and they staggered back to their camps, fighting all the way.

As he turned into Stocks Green Road, he noticed through the gloom a figure ahead. There was something strange about him. His smart clothing was dishevelled, and his gait was slow, as if he were dragging a heavy weight. Yank was now level with him and as he was about to bid him good evening, the man staggered and nearly fell into the roadside ditch. Giving a cry, then a moan, he hit the muddy ground and lay there unable to move.

Yank attempted to get the lad to stand, for he could see, even in the September light, that he was young. The boy gave another cry as he tried to struggle to his feet.

"Now, what you doing out after dark on your own?" He studied the lad as he stood slightly crouched. He was clearly distressed. "Are you hurt? Do you live round here?"

Still no answer, though the boy seemed to understand the question by the way he slowly moved his head from one side to the other, his hand to his forehead.

"You'll die of cold if you don't get some shelter soon. Can I take you home?"

"No, no! No, don't take me back. No!"

Ah, a runaway. "Can you walk? What's your name?" Yank picked up a bundle of clothes, which confirmed to him the lad was trying to escape from somewhere or someone.

"It's Tob... Thomas."

Yank noticed the hesitation. If that wasn't his name, he had enough about him not to reveal what it was.

"Well, Thomas. What can I do to help?"

"Your voice, it's... it's not from this country, is it?"

"I'm from New York. Do you know where that is?"

"Across the Atlantic."

This boy was well read; his voice told Yank that as well as his knowledge. How strange.

"Yes."

"Can I stay with you, sir, please? I don't know what to do, where to go." His eyes, streaked with tears of fear, stared up at Yank.

"I don't think so. I only rent a room, and my landlady hasn't any others available."

"I have some money." He patted a pocket in his overcoat.

"Shush," Yank said quickly. "Keep that quiet or you'll not have it for long. The men round here are very rough."

"I know, I hid behind a tree when I saw some men and boys earlier," Thomas said, grimacing. "They were disgusting – filthy, dirty and speaking horrible words I couldn't understand."

"How did you know they were horrible words, then?" Yank kept him talking while he tried to work out how he could best deal with the situation. It would not be smart to leave him, especially so near the beer house; the navvies would pounce on such a personable looking young man, strip him of his clothes and beat him up just for the hell of it.

"I just know, sir," Thomas said. "It was the way they laughed."

Yank grinned. "Call me Yank, everyone does. Now, are you strong enough to walk with me? I'll see if you can share my room for the night, but I'm not sure I'll succeed 'cause my landlady's not very—"

Thomas swayed and seemed about to fall.

"Here, lean on me, it's a tidy way to my lodging, almost into Leigh."

With Thomas holding his arm, they walked slowly along the dark road. It had been cloudy all day and that night was darker than usual. Several times the boy made a sound, something between a grunt and a cry. Exhaustion, Yank supposed.

"How do you see where you're going?" the boy asked. "I can see nothing at all. I would have fallen if you hadn't caught me. When darkness came a few hours ago, I did fall into a ditch."

"I can have a lantern, but I've got used to it now and I know the road. You've never been out in the dark, have you?"

Though Yank could barely see the boy's face, he sensed the shake of his head. He could try Mrs Grimley, he guessed, but she sure wasn't a woman who took kindly to anyone, let alone those who worked on the new railway. *"Spoiling the countryside – I don't like it. Nothing good will come of it, you mark my words. And those navvies, dreadful they are."*

Yank didn't know how he had managed to persuade her to take him in the first place, for he had told her he was a bricklayer with the new railway right from the beginning. He must have put on his most charming smile for she said he could have a room for four shillings a week, which he thought was high; a whole house could be rented for that. He was about to bargain, but decided he was not in a good position to do so, and she had mentioned providing food.

As expected, his landlady was not accommodating and adamantly refused to let Thomas in the house.

"He's one of them navvies, ain't he, Mr Yank?" She stood glaring, hands on her ample hips, from the doorway of her terraced cottage. She was wearing a long, black tweed skirt, which was covered by a dirty, originally white apron, and a shirt of a nondescript colour. Round her shoulders was a woollen shawl, the ends of which were tucked into her skirt. Her grey hair was pulled back from her face.

"No, he isn't."

"Then what's 'e doing wandering 'bout these parts at night? Asking for trouble, that's what."

"I thought so too, ma'am," he said in a conciliatory voice. "I knew you'd understand. This young boy has… has lost his way. You can see he has decent clothes." He urged Thomas forward so she could see him in the candlelight. He turned to Thomas, who was grimacing. "Tell Mrs Grimley."

"I'm very tired and I would be no trouble. I can pay you."

The landlady's eyes lit up. "How much you got, then?"

"That's a private matter. If he's going to share my room, he needn't pay anything." Yank knew he was on shaky ground, but he hated the way she was trying to take advantage of the boy.

"Oh, very well, come in, then." She stood aside.

"Do you think… would you mind… could I have a drink of water?"

Yank tut-tutted, upset with himself. Of course, if he had run away, it was doubtful he'd had anything to eat or drink for some time. As Yank wasn't sure where Thomas had come from or when he had left his home, he couldn't work out how long he had been on the road.

Yank looked at Mrs Grimley. "I'll get him some water." As he passed her, he whispered in her ear. "Perhaps you could find him a crust of bread."

Thomas gulped down the water and ate the bread ravenously. Yank looked on, frowning, but Mrs Grimley lived up to her name.

"You can stay, two shillings for the week, then you'll have to find somewhere else."

Yank wasn't going to let her get away with that, but for now it was the best he could hope for. "Thank you, ma'am. Perhaps you might have a palliasse that the boy can sleep on, or something not too hard."

"I don't know 'bout that. Next you'll be wanting a proper bed."

"That's a good idea." With that, Yank hurried to the door beside the range. He lifted the latch and, urging the weary Thomas in front of him, they went up the curved wooden staircase.

"There's one in the cupboard on the landing," Mrs Grimley shouted.

* * *

Next morning, Yank woke early and lay listening to the bird song and distant church bells. He had to think what to do about Thomas. Should he try to return him home? The lad was adamant he didn't want to go back. He was lying on his side on the floor beside his bed, a rough blanket partly covering him. Yank watched as he turned on his face and the tail of his shirt slightly rode up his body.

Yank gasped. There were great wheals across the boy's back in recent, bloody stripes. Some had dried, some were weeping with pus. His shirt was blood-soaked and was stuck to his back in places. Why hadn't he noticed this last night when he had taken off his coat? Yank, recalling how gingerly Thomas had removed it, now saw the reason for the grunts and cries he had made during their walk here.

"Who did that?" he shouted.

Thomas woke with a start. The sudden movement as he sat up brought tears to his eyes as his wounds opened and bled.

"Who did that?" Yank repeated.

"Did what?"

"You know what; someone has beaten you, badly. Who did such a thing? Was it those people you said you'd seen?" Yank was used to seeing severe cuts, bruises, broken bones and gaping wounds, most of them caused by fights or accidents on the railway: but this was deliberate and brutal and not likely to have been done by a navvy. "Who beat you like that?" he demanded.

"You won't send me back, will you – if I tell you?"

Yank shook his head emphatically. "No."

"It was my father."

Chapter Two

Septimus Laird stood in the parlour of his well-appointed house in the north of the small market town of Tunbridge, in the county of Kent. Sitting beside him was his wife, a small, pallid woman in her early thirties, who looked in her mid-forties. Assembled were their seven children and five live-in servants.

They stood to attention as Septimus Laird, elder of the church and a notable man of the town, was about to take morning prayers.

"Sit down," he boomed. "The reading this morning is taken from St Paul's First Epistle to the Corinthians, Chapter Seven, Verse One."

He began to read. "'Now concerning the things whereof you wrote to me: it is good for a man not to touch a woman. Nevertheless, to avoid fornication, let every man have his own wife, and let every woman have her own husband. Let every husband render unto the wife due benevolence and likewise also the wife unto the husband…'"

"Father, what's fornication?" Elizabeth, his eldest daughter, looked at her father enquiringly.

"Don't interrupt," he snapped.

"But how can I tell what the verses mean if you don't tell me what the words mean?"

Her father's face began to redden.

"I was thinking the same, Father," said Tobias, Elizabeth's older brother, hoping to help out his sister. He realised she was being provocative, though he wasn't sure whether this was deliberate or not. "You tell us to read the Bible every day, which I do, but I don't always understand."

"Both of you up to your rooms immediately. I will not have prayers disrupted in this manner."

At the sound of harsh, loud words, the baby, who was being held in the nursemaid's arms, started to cry.

"Take that child out!"

The nurse began cooing and rocking the baby in her arms, but to no avail. She trembled as she saw the master becoming more and more infuriated.

Mrs Laird stood up. "Give her to me."

Thankfully, the nurse went over to Mrs Laird and placed the crying baby in her arms.

"It's not your job to quieten the child, Amelia. That's what *she's* here for."

"I'll take her, Septimus, and then you can complete prayers in peace." With that she left the parlour, followed by the relieved nursemaid.

Tobias, Elizabeth and James, their brother, watched in amazement. This was the most defiant they had ever seen their mama. Their father continued his reading as Tobias and Elizabeth left the room.

"Look, Lizzie, don't upset Father by arguing," Tobias urged, as they both went into the upstairs bedroom Tobias shared with James.

"But *you* do."

"Yes, I know, but I can stand the beatings better than you."

"I don't care. It was perfectly reasonable to ask, and why shouldn't a man touch a woman? People touch each other every day."

"Yes, but you know he doesn't like to be questioned in any respect, however reasonable. Promise me?"

"Oh, very well, but it's so unfair. I wish I could leave this horrible house."

Tobias wished the same. He had often thought about it. But what would he do? How would he live? Could he earn any money? If so, doing what? Could he leave his brothers and sisters, not to mention his dear mama?

They heard their father mounting the stairs.

"Why are you here and not in your own room as I ordered?" he said to Elizabeth, waving his cane.

"I wanted to be with Tobias. We both asked the same question so you can give us the answer together." She was about to say it would save time but heeded her brother's advice and clamped her mouth shut.

Her defiance left her father apoplectic. He raised his cane and ordered Elizabeth to put out her hand.

"Don't, Father. She's done nothing wrong and neither have I. We just wanted to know what the word meant. What's wrong with that?"

"You do as you're told. Hold out your hand, young lady." Thomas stood in front of his sister. "You're not to touch her. Give me her punishment."

"How dare you!" his father shouted. "How dare you challenge my authority?" He pushed Tobias so violently he fell to the floor and banged his head on the brass bedstead. Septimus grabbed Elizabeth's hand. Tobias leapt up and grasped the cane, wrestling it from his father's hand. He then put it across his raised knee and snapped it in half.

"Don't touch her! Don't touch Elizabeth, or any of the girls. Not Jane, nor Emma or baby Charlotte. If you do, I shall stop you."

Tobias was trembling, not only with anger but with fear. Beatings were a part of life and were to be expected if something wrong had been done, but his father was a bully, and he was sure he enjoyed the suffering of the people under his control.

Mr Laird stared at his children, turned and left the room, slamming the door behind him.

Tobias put his arm around his sister's shoulders. "Are you all right, Lizzie?"

"Did you really do that – break the cane?" She looked at the broken pieces on the rug. "What will he do to us? I'm scared."

"He won't touch me again, don't worry." He pulled back his shoulders defiantly.

But his father had means of retaliating that Tobias knew nothing about. He was soon to find out what these were; and being strong and tall for fourteen was not going to help him.

Tobias was fast asleep, but he woke suddenly. His father was pulling him from the bed. He was still not fully awake as he was dragged, stumbling, down the stairs and into his father's study. He glanced around the room and his eyes alighted on the leather razor strop that was lying on his father's desk. With great fear, he realised his fate. Despite his former resolve, he was powerless.

An hour later, Tobias felt able to get up onto his knees. He stood gingerly and despite feeling dizzy and sick, managed to crawl slowly, inch by painful inch, up the stairs to his bedroom. Quietly, so as not to disturb James, he searched his drawers for as many clothes as he thought he could carry and bundled them into a shirt. He felt in the wardrobe for his coat and found five shillings that he had managed to squirrel away over the years from money an aunt had given him. The children usually had any money they received as presents taken from them to put in the collection at Sunday church.

Tobias crept down to the hall and through the kitchen. Tears streamed down his face from the excruciating pain in his back. Tilda, the scullery maid, was snoring on the truckle bed beside the range. Thankfully, she did not stir. He didn't want her to know anything about this episode, though either way, she would probably be held responsible.

Yank burst through the door at the bottom of the stairs, dragging poor Thomas behind him. A startled Mrs Grimley nearly dropped the cup she was holding.

"Look at this!" In his anger, he pulled Thomas forward none too gently. "Just look at this." He turned Thomas around and lifted his shirt, causing the boy to cry out as it caught a forming scab.

Mrs Grimley gasped. "Who did—?"

"It was his father." Yank was beside himself with rage.

"Oh, you poor boy." She looked at Yank. "That needs some attention. Shall we get a doctor?"

"No, no!" Thomas pleaded.

Yank understood. Thomas could think a doctor might know him, or if not then recall him when it was known he was a runaway.

"No, but I guess we could do something. Have you any suggestions, ma'am?"

"Well, Mr Yank, my mother used to put salt on our cuts. It didn't half hurt, but it seemed to do the trick. Let's bathe his back with warm salt water. The kettle's steaming on the hob."

She filled a small tin basin, added cold water to the hot, put in a teaspoon of salt and dipped a piece of rag into it.

"Now, Thomas, Mr Yank will help you take off your shirt; it's covered in blood anyway. Have you got another in your bundle?"

Thomas nodded.

"You bend over the table, and I'll wash your cuts. It's going to sting, I warn you."

Yank held Thomas's hand while Mrs Grimley ministered to him. The boy winced and jumped several times, but though Yank saw tears trickle from his tightly shut eyes, he never once cried out.

James woke with a start and immediately sensed something was wrong. He looked over to Tobias's bed. It was empty. A drawer of the chest was half open with a garment partly showing. He went to Elizabeth's bedroom, even though his father disapproved.

"Lizzie," he whispered, in case she was still asleep. "Is Tobias here?"

It was Jane, his younger sister, who replied. "No, he isn't here. What's wrong?"

Sleepily, Elizabeth said, "What about Tobias?"

"He isn't in our bedroom. There's something wrong, I know it. I think he's run away." The grandfather clock struck six-thirty. "I'm going downstairs."

In the kitchen, the servants were busy; cook was preparing breakfast with the help of the kitchen maid; the nursemaid was preparing milk for the baby and the housemaid was getting hot water ready to take up to the bedrooms.

"Hello, Master James. Too hungry to wait for breakfast?" Cook laughed.

"Have you seen Tobias? He's not in our bedroom."

They all looked at each other, puzzled. "No," they murmured, slowly shaking their heads.

James followed the housemaid, who was carrying two big copper jugs up the stairs. She went along the landing to the master's bedroom and knocked. A bellow instructed her to "come". She wondered whether to tell Mr Laird that Tobias was missing, but she was too fearful.

At breakfast, when they were all seated, Mr Laird enquired of James why Tobias was not yet down. James explained that he could not be found, and then he waited for his father's usual response to anything that did not meet with his approval. James was sure his brother's disappearance would be considered his fault.

"Have you done something to him?" Amelia asked her husband. She thought maybe he had shut him in another room, or even in the shed. She recalled the trouble at morning prayers yesterday and the filthy temper he had been in since. Septimus was going too far. She pursed her lips as he left the room, and they heard him loudly mount the stairs, shouting Tobias's name. When he returned, his face was still red, but surprisingly he seemed less irate and wore a worried frown. "That boy must be found," he exclaimed.

Elizabeth was about to ask where they were going to search for him, but again remembered what Tobias had said about annoying her father.

Down in the kitchen, the servants, aware of the master's temper, were also discussing the turn of events.

"Tilda, did you hear anything while you were in the kitchen overnight?" asked Cook.

"I didn't hear nuffin'. Nobody came through here dat I knows 'bout."

"You know, Cook," the housemaid said, "when I was laying the fire in the study this morning, I saw a spot of blood on the carpet."

"Perhaps he's been murdered!" said Tilda, hugging herself.

"Don't be so silly, girl! Who'd want to murder Master Tobias? And where's his body? Do you think the murderer also dug a hole in the garden and buried him? Get on with what you were doing."

Nevertheless, they were all disturbed by the disappearance. Tobias was liked by all the servants, and they knew he mostly bore the brunt of his father's ill temper.

In his study, Mr Laird ranted to his wife about the boy and his disobedience, lack of respect and absence of concern for the worry he was causing. "He must be found," he reiterated. "I'll talk to the servants. They might know something." He stroked his whiskers. "I can get Dawkins to saddle the horse and go looking for him. He can't have gone far."

"And what do you suppose made him leave?" She stared at her husband. "And where would he go? He must have been very upset to have done such a drastic thing. I think we ought to call someone in authority."

"Certainly not, I'll deal with this." He pensively stood up.

"You're too strict with the children. It has to stop." Her eyes began to fill with tears. It was terrible to think of her son wandering around in the night. He had no idea what sort of people he might come across, especially with all the upset of the new railway. The boy had never been out by himself.

"Amelia, I will not have you speaking to me in that manner. I expect to be obeyed and you must do as I say."

Amelia left the room with a swish of her grey, taffeta gown and loudly slammed the door.

Chapter Three

IT WAS NEARLY three weeks since Thomas had arrived at Mrs Grimley's. Much to Yank's amusement and surprise, she seemed to have turned into a new person and was protective of the boy, whom she now saw as her sole responsibility. She had no children, so maybe she was treating him as the child she never had.

Thomas had been feverish and, when he wasn't having his wounds bathed, he spent a great deal of time asleep on Yank's bed. Yank had to leave for work by seven o'clock, and most evenings he did not return until late, working by lantern if necessary. The sub-contractor on this stretch of line was determined that work should go on until the men dropped. No wonder the navvies spent all their money on drink. Thankfully, Yank was not under the direct jurisdiction of a sub-contractor. As a bricklayer on bridges, tunnels and stations, he was employed directly by South Eastern Railway. Nevertheless, bricklaying had to keep up to speed.

"How're you feeling, Thomas?" Yank asked that evening.

"He's much, much better," Mrs Grimley replied for him. "There are scabs now, and they only bleed if he catches them."

"Now," Yank began, as they sat at the bare wooden table, eating the evening meal of meat and vegetables, "we have to decide what's to be done."

"He can stay here," his landlady said, giving the boy a benign smile.

"Yes, that's kind of you, but people will be looking for him." He turned to Thomas. "Did you say your family has servants?"

"Yes, five in the house and a groom who lives over the stable. Oh, and a gardener comes in four days a week."

Neither Mrs Grimley nor Yank had ever had anything to do with people in such exalted positions. They looked at each other, unable to find words to express their thoughts, their lips clamped in a thin line. Mrs Grimley gathered up some dishes and went into the scullery.

"What do you think your father will do, or has done already?" Yank asked. "He could be sending the servants out to look for you."

"I don't know. He's probably glad I've gone."

Yank thought this extremely unlikely. The disgrace of having your son run away would be more than a man of Mr Laird's description could stand. What excuse would he give for a missing son? Anyway, he was sure the servants would talk – there were enough of them.

"Could you find me some work? I'm quite strong, you know – now I'm nearly better." He looked pleadingly at Yank.

"How old are you? Sixteen?"

"Er, fourteen."

"Goodness! You are tall for your age."

Thomas sat up proudly, though a catching scab made him wince. "What about building the new railway? I've read all about it in the *Maidstone Journal* and *The Times*. They need lots of men and boys."

Yank smiled. "They reckon it even takes a labourer on the land – and they're used to hard graft – a year to be anywhere near a match for the type of work they have you do. You wouldn't last five minutes. Look at your hands."

Thomas held them out and Yank put his coarse, calloused hands, with their short, chipped nails ringed with red brick dust, beside Thomas's snowy white and unblemished ones. "And I don't have to shovel earth all day long. I don't think even I could do it, certainly not all day."

"But what about the boys?"

"Well, I grant you, they don't have to do much

hard digging with shovels and pickaxes, but they run up and down all day long with barrows they've filled with earth. They hardly have a break. You wouldn't be able to deal with it."

Thomas looked sceptical and clearly didn't believe him.

Mrs Grimley came back into the room from the scullery with three apples. "What wouldn't he be able to deal with?"

"Working on the railway."

"I should think not. He's much too gentle a boy to be mixing with those terrible men." She screwed up her nose.

"I mix with those sorts of people, ma'am," protested Yank.

"Ah, but you're different." Mrs Grimley replied.

"But I can't stay here, cause I haven't enough money," Thomas said.

"Never mind that. Anyway, you're not better yet." She picked up their three bowls and swept back into the scullery.

Yank and Thomas smiled at each other. "You certainly seem to have worked magic on that lady."

He was called Big Yank. Why *big* no one knew, because he wasn't particularly tall. He was the only American the working mates had ever come across, and everyone seemed to have some sort of nickname. It was known he was born in New York, and a few of his workmates knew this was in America, and that America was across an ocean and a long way away. Several of the Irish had relatives who had immigrated there, so they were a little more knowledgeable.

Most would not remember exactly when Big Yank joined them. There was so much bricklaying to be done between Tunbridge and Red Hill village, and beyond those locations he could have joined almost anywhere on that part of the line, which was eventually to end at Dover. Although not actually a navvy, his workmates considered him one of them, yet he remained a loner. He was friendly, worked hard and drank with them occasionally, but he was never seen drunk. He had no wife or woman with him and always rented lodgings rather than doss down in the huts, tents and other makeshift dwellings the navvies made for themselves beside the track. One of their camps was at Leigh, a village some seven miles from Tunbridge. If everything went to schedule, the line to that market town was due to open sometime next year, in 1841.

Yank had learned his trade in New York. He started at twelve, which was younger than Thomas, but by then he was already more worldly. After his apprenticeship he worked for a while on the city's new railways, but he fancied his chances in England, arriving in Liverpool, where railway building was booming. After a couple of years, his restless nature drove him south and he joined the gangs building the permanent way for the newly formed South Eastern Railway.

This line was set to go east from the new London/Brighton line and continue through Tunbridge, Ashford and on to Dover, thus providing the important link to the continent. It was being built in sections simultaneously, each with its own contractor or sub-contractor. At Reigate, where the South Eastern Railway was to branch east, there would be a station at a little village called Red Hill. At present, Yank was working on the bridge at Leigh, where the railway was going over the road. There would, he knew, be plenty of work for a bricklayer for many years to come.

Yank continued to worry about Thomas. Both he and Mrs Grimley would be in serious trouble if it were discovered they were sheltering a known runaway, for there was no way they could disguise this fact. For his part, Thomas was convinced he could lose himself amongst the workers. He obviously hadn't learned from those he had already encountered or from what Yank had tried to impress upon him.

One Sunday morning, Thomas was eating his breakfast of bread and an egg when he faintly heard the church bells. "It's Sunday!" he suddenly announced. "I must go to church."

Yank and Mrs Grimley glanced at each other, a frown clouding their faces. Why had he suddenly thought that? He must have heard the church bells on previous Sundays.

"That's out of the question," said Yank. "You know that. You mustn't be seen – well, not yet. You must be careful."

Thomas realised how silly he was being and lowered his eyes. Why hadn't he noticed the church bells before? His family would be going into the town about now. He felt a lump in his throat.

Yank pushed his plate away and stood up. "I'm going to take you to the camp on the green. You come from a…" He was going to say how sheltered Thomas's life had been, but Thomas must realise that for himself. The sentence lay unfinished.

They tried to dress him in a manner that would not make him stand out, but this proved more difficult than Yank had first thought. His landlady had washed Thomas's few items of clothing, something else that surprised Yank. "It's no good, we shall have to make some of his clothes dirty," he said.

"What! After all the trouble I've gone to," grumbled Mrs Grimley.

"Well, what do you suggest? He can't go out as if he were about to attend church. He'd stand out where I'm going to take him."

"Not to that disgusting camp, I hope."

"Yes, ma'am, that's just what I am going to do. If he's going to be 'lost', he's got to learn what it's like to live like many people building the railway do." *Like most people do*, he guessed, *whether building a railway or not.*

Yank was troubled and constantly trying to think how to manage Thomas's new life. Recently, his overseer had remonstrated with him about his concentration, to which Yank had not taken kindly, because he was careful over his work.

"Give me your trousers and I'll rub them in the earth, and the shirt you've got on. It's already bloodstained."

Mrs Grimley was outraged. "I spent ages trying to get that out," she complained.

"I'm not criticising your washing, ma'am. I just want him to look like the rest of us. As it is, his shirt and trousers are of very good quality."

Thomas listened, frowning. How different his life was from most people's. He knew there were poor people, his father was always complaining about them, but he was sure his father had no idea how they lived and worked because he would not deign to find out. It would be their fault they were poor in the first place.

They set off at a brisk pace. Thomas found that Yank snapped answers when he spoke; not that he was anything like his father in a bad temper, but Yank had been so kind and gentle until now that it upset him. Long-legged as he was, he had to jog to keep up.

The smell reached him first as they approached Leigh Green. The surrounding fields were a mass of ramshackle buildings on churned-up mud. The first shack they approached had been put together with corrugated iron, three wooden planks and a hoarding advertising cheese. Two pieces of canvas had been thrown over the top, which just about covered the roof. On top of this, keeping the canvas in place, was turf. Another frayed length of canvas had been hung over the front. The entire structure was no more than seven or eight square feet. A child of about three was sitting in the mud nearby eating a piece of bread.

"See that," said Yank, "probably three or four people live in there."

"But they couldn't possibly all lie down together."

"They probably take it in turns to sleep – or sleep sitting up. That kid, if it belongs to that hut, most likely sleeps on a shelf."

"Can one sleep sitting up?"

"You can do anything if you haven't any other means."

"Don't often see you 'ere, Big Yank," someone called.

Thomas jumped and turned to see a man whose clothes were so filthy he was sure they would stand up on their own should he take them off. The man's moleskin trousers were held up with a thick belt, but

Thomas couldn't discern the colour of the shirt under his waistcoat. A red kerchief, at least Thomas thought it was originally red, was tied round his neck, and on his feet were hobnailed boots thickly covered in mud. Mr Jim, his father's gardener, looked better than this.

"This one of yourn we don't know 'bout?" the man said, a grin on his face.

"No, Smithy Joe, he's a… a relation of my landlady, wanted to see how you lived. He comes from, er, London." Yank thought how careful he constantly had to be to cover up Thomas's position.

"Well, young'un, what d'yer think?"

Yank turned his head away and whispered, "You're not educated, remember."

Thomas obliged. "Dunno, bit crahded, and smells a bit."

The men both laughed.

"That was fantastic, Thomas," Yank said as they moved away. "You sounded, well, just right. How d'you do it?"

Thomas swelled with pride. "It's how our gardener speaks; he comes from London."

Nobody had ever praised him, not even his tutor. He would do anything for Yank. How fortunate he was to have found someone like him; kind, thoughtful and literate. He had seen some simple books on the shelf in the bedroom, though Yank didn't have much time for reading because he worked so hard and was exhausted when he got back in the evenings. Thomas knew he went out for a drink sometimes because that was how he met him, but Yank had not been out since Thomas had been staying at Mrs Grimley's.

They moved on, Thomas feeling quite sick with the stench. How could they live like that?

"What do you think of the smell?" Yank asked, seeing the disgust on Thomas's face. "Most of the men rarely wash properly 'cause there's no running water; neither do they wash their clothes, as you could see. You know, in America, they call railway labourers 'boomers' or 'thousand-mile shirts' because they travel light and wear the same clothes all the time."

"They don't actually wear them for that long, do they?" Thomas stared in disbelief.

Yank smiled. "Wouldn't be surprised. When I worked in the north of England, I heard of one man who, it was said, had never taken his hat off, ever."

"No, surely not." Thomas paused. "It's quite quiet, isn't it? Where is everybody?"

"Not in church, I can assure you. They've been drinking most of yesterday evening and are sleeping it off. In some parts of the country, after they've been paid for the month, they go on what's called a randy and don't work for one or two days because they're not capable. On this stretch of the line, they get paid weekly; that way they haven't so much money in their pockets, and they don't get quite so drunk."

Chapter Four

HAVING TAKEN Thomas to the camp on Sunday, Yank now wanted to show him first-hand what working on the railway involved. He knew the boy hadn't believed a word he'd said about what the young lads and labourers did, and how hard it was.

"It may take me some time, Yank," Thomas had said, "but I'll get there in the end, you'll see. I'll earn some money, and then I can pay Mrs Grimley and stay with you for good."

Yank ignored this grand talk. The boy simply could not believe the trouble he was in – the trouble they were all in.

"I want you up by six-thirty, Thomas, and you can come with me to see what work you think you can do."

Mrs Grimley was appalled. She pleaded with Yank not to take him, and certainly not to let him work with those dreadful people. The trouble was, like Thomas, she didn't think beyond the moment. Thomas was still a runaway and could be discovered at any moment, for they had now gathered they were close to his home – Thomas had let slip that he lived in the north of Tunbridge, near a windmill. If Yank did not find some way of hiding him, even if not as a railway boy, then he'd have to think of something else. It was the 'something else' that was most worrying.

Yank took Thomas to an area not far from where he was working on the bridge in Leigh. "Railways must run on land as flat as possible: no steep gradients. Do you know what a gradient is, Thomas?"

"Of course," he said, indignant.

Yank grinned. "Of course," he muttered to himself before continuing. "So, if the land is not reasonably flat, there must be bridges over or under the road. If the land isn't deep enough for cuttings there are embankments. That's what these labourers are doing."

Yank waved his hand towards the boys scurrying up and down like ants. He called to a sturdy, well-built boy, his hobnailed boots thick with mud to his ankles. "Hey, you lad! Come here a minute."

"Canna stop long cuz ah be in trouble. Whas tha want?"

"Can you tell this lad from London what you're doing?"

The boy thought it was obvious, but he said scornfully, and in a monotone, "I 'as ta fill barrow wi' earth from where we're told and take it t' top of yon 'bankment along the track til it reaches the reet height."

"Here, Thomas, push this lad's barrow over there." Yank pointed to a spot about two yards away.

The boy laughed, realising what Yank was trying to prove. Thomas confidently grasped the handles and strained to take the weight. He looked to see if something was in its way.

"That sure is heavy clay in there," Yank said. "This part of Kent is renowned for its clay soil. In London, it's even worse. The great engineer George Stephenson said that clay would rather go up hill than stand still. And if it isn't clay, it's rock that must be drilled and blasted through. They've had to do that near Dover. Then it all needs shifting." He looked at Thomas and shook his head sadly. "You wouldn't last two minutes."

Undeterred, Thomas turned to the boy for a second opinion. "I would get better, wouldn't I?"

The lad could tell Thomas wasn't the rough sort they were. "Nay," he said.

"Well, who's in charge of you? I might be able to do something else," Thomas said belligerently, not wishing to be put off, and forgetting he had to speak in an uneducated manner.

Yank thanked the boy, who turned, picked up the

handles of the barrow as if it were near empty, and pushed it up to the top of the embankment, where he tipped the contents out before rushing down to where further mounds of earth, brought by others from previous cuttings, were awaiting dispersal.

"I could hardly understand a word he said. Where's he come from?" Thomas asked.

"Lancashire or Derbyshire possibly; maybe Staffordshire. I've heard the accents, but I can't always tell where they come from. There are many workers down here from the north, and some Irish."

"Is there *anything* I can do?" Thomas said, near to tears. "No one would come searching for me here amongst these people, would they?"

"That's true, I guess, but you're just not strong enough and the men and boys would know that. You would be teased mercilessly or brought into fights deliberately whether you wanted to be or not. You'd probably be beaten up just because you are who you are." Yank was desperate for Thomas to understand his limitations. "And another thing, Thomas, work on the railway is very dangerous: there is a lot of gunpowder around, with constant blasting and accidental explosions. Why, just recently, here in Leigh, three men were injured by pieces of stone that shattered from an explosion. One of them didn't survive. No, we must think of some other way. I must go now. Can you find your way back all right?"

"Yes, I suppose so."

Thomas watched, disconsolately, as Yank strode away from him. He wanted to see the bridge Yank was working on in Leigh and what bricklaying he had to do, but he guessed he had done enough for him.

From a distance, he watched the workers for a while, marvelling at the strength and speed of the boys and the sheer strength of the navvies, who wielded their pickaxes and shovelled the heavy soil as if it were no heavier than snow. He had always been interested in the building of the railways and was excited when he heard it was coming to his town. It was not like the railways in the north: there were no big industries down here. Thomas had read that this line was being constructed because of its closeness to France and the rest of the continent. He thought railways were a very good idea, though most of his parents' friends were appalled at the desecration of the countryside and wondered at the landowners allowing the tracks to go over their estates. Thomas, however, wondered how much they were getting paid. They certainly wouldn't let the South Eastern Railway have their land for nothing. As far as Thomas understood it, the landowners could make a great deal of money and probably (now he was really thinking like a landowner) said they didn't want to sell up in order to extract yet more money. He suddenly recalled another reason why his father was so against it; he had shares in the Turnpike Trust, which collected money from people using toll roads. If goods and people travelled by train, these toll roads would no longer be needed.

Thomas turned his back on the railway activity and began retracing his steps. Before leaving Leigh to go back to Mrs Grimley, he saw a hurdy-gurdy man with a monkey on his shoulder. He was standing outside the church and several children had gathered around him, clearly as fascinated as Thomas was. He had never seen such a person and certainly not a monkey, even though he had seen them in picture books. When the man finished turning the handle on his instrument, the music stopped, and when all the children had drifted away, Thomas went up to him and asked if he could touch the monkey. He nodded, and Thomas tentatively put out his hand and stroked the animal. The man smiled at the boy and said, "Here, give him this banana."

As with the monkey, Thomas had only seen a banana in pictures and was fascinated as he watched the monkey peel and then eat the fruit.

One evening, Mr Laird called all the servants into his study. Even the kitchen maid was summoned, much to Cook's surprise.

"I have called you here because, as you know... um, my son has disappeared from the house. I do not know why this has happened – perhaps he has got into some bad company and has been led astray."

Dawkins, the groom, gave a grunt; the boy hardly left the house and then was never alone.

Mr Laird glared at him. "I want the boy found," he said, "and I'm offering a reward of a shilling for any information and, er, four shillings for whoever finds him."

Dawkins' eyes lit up. He could already feel the money in his pocket; the largest coin he had ever seen was a gold and shiny guinea.

He wondered why Mr Laird never called his son by name. Was he ashamed of him? He'd heard that all the children were treated harshly. Master Tobias had probably run away because his father had beaten him once too often. Still, four shillings was four shillings. He was sure the boy could be found.

Mr Laird resumed his speech. "I am going to let Dawkins have the horse so he can cover more ground, and he is more likely to see or hear something. The rest of you must listen to any gossip at the shops or amongst your friends on your afternoon off."

He dismissed them but asked the groom to remain. "Perhaps you could ask the gardener to keep his ear to the ground, Dawkins – and your wife, too."

"Yes, sir, if you don't need the trap or carriage, I can start straight away."

* * *

Within half an hour, Dawkins had Ember saddled and was off. After considering which direction he should attempt, he had decided through the town towards Southborough would be his best bet. He didn't think Master Tobias would have got very far, and he was bound to be avoiding the navvies because of their filthy and offensive way of living, even though they seemed to be everywhere.

It was Tuesday, market day, and the main street was teeming with cattle and farm labourers, switches in hand, trying to keep some sort of order as they travelled to or from the market. In addition, wagons full of materials for the new railway, off-loaded at Medway Wharf, competed for space with the cows, sheep and pigs. Even Dawkins, who considered the coming railway a good idea, wondered if the chaos would ever end. He slowly manoeuvred his way along Bridge Street, fording the streams that crossed the road. He reached the area where the railway and the turnpike met, near the ruins of the Priory. There, crossing the road already, were rails bolted to boards, which could be removed to aid the railway building. He looked around before climbing up Quarry Hill. The lad wasn't worldly wise and would be sleeping rough and trying to find food. He would make enquiries at the various beer houses and hostelries along the way. Master Tobias might have asked for food somewhere, and his clothes would give him away. He wondered if the boy had any money with him and decided it was unlikely.

By the time he reached the outskirts of Southborough, he had neither seen nor heard anything that might give a clue to the boy's whereabouts. Disappointed, he turned the horse and slowly rode back the way he'd come, peering into the hedges on either side of the road. He stopped a filthy, ragged-clothed boy near the turnpike and described Tobias to him, but he was told there were so many boys working on the railway that he wouldn't know who was or wasn't. Dawkins frowned. It set him thinking that maybe Master Tobias was wiser than he thought. Where better to lose yourself than amongst the workers on the railway?

Elizabeth was crying. She cried a great deal lately but tried not to let her father see her. She missed her brother so much; they often talked about their lessons, or what was in the newspapers. What she didn't understand she asked him to explain. Life without him was intolerable. True, her father had not been so harsh recently. He rarely asked their tutor, Mr Hargreaves, how she was progressing, which meant she avoided being hit when it was reported back she had not quite grasped something. Mr Hargreaves often seemed as ill-tempered as her father, though she and Tobias had to admit he was a good teacher, and they mostly enjoyed their lessons.

Where had Tobias gone? What had made him leave so suddenly? He had not spoken to her about running away. What had happened? Elizabeth wanted to discuss this with her mother, but she also spent hours weeping. The atmosphere in the house was strange, not oppressive as usual, but sad and mysterious, as if something were not being said. Why had her father called the servants together and what did he say? The only person she thought she could ask was Tilda. When she had finished her lessons for the day, she went to look for her.

Elizabeth found the kitchen maid in the garden emptying the vegetable peelings. She was lucky to catch her on her own, as Cook kept a careful watch over her.

"Tilda, what did my father have to say this morning?"

"He, um, he, um… wanted us to find Master Tobias," she stuttered, a little frightened of Miss Elizabeth.

"What, to go and look for him? Does he know where he's gone, then?"

"Oh, no. No one knows where 'e's gone. We could have a shilling he said, if we found out anyfin'. He said perhaps he had been led astray."

"Led astray! Where on earth would he find anyone to lead him astray?"

"Dunno. I don't know what 'led astray' means, but dat's what the Master said." Being able to provide Miss Elizabeth with information made Tilda feel important. She then added, her finger pointing in the air as she remembered, "He did say Dawkins could have the horse, and he wanted the rest of us to listen for any talk. But I don't go out—"

"Did my father say where he thought my brother had gone?"

Tilda shook her head.

Elizabeth grasped the fingers of one hand, squeezing them tightly as she digested this information. "Thank you, Tilda, that's all for now. Oh, and don't tell anyone I've spoken to you, and if you find out anything – anything – tell me as soon as possible. Understand?" She glared at the girl, hoping this would frighten her sufficiently to heed her instructions.

Later that morning, when Elizabeth spotted the gardener outside, she flew down the path, where he was dealing with some dead and dying shrubs, some clippings at his feet. "Mr Jim. Did you know that my brother is missing?"

"Yes, Miss Elizabeth, Dawkins told me. It's Master Tobias, isn't it, not James or your other brother?"

"No, not them. He wasn't at breakfast one morning, and he hasn't been seen since. No one knows where he's gone, and the servants have been told to try and find out. Dawkins is out now looking for him." She began to cry. "I think my father did something to him. He's offering money if any of the servants can help."

"There, Miss Elizabeth, don't cry. He's sure to turn up. I'll look out for him and ask me friends to do the same. He won't have got far now, will he?"

Jim tried to cheer her up, but he was as distressed as she was. He thought Master Tobias was an extremely bright young lad, very polite and interested in everything. He wasn't sure what went on between him and his father, but from time to time he had noticed bruises on the youngster's face and arms. From his own experience, he certainly knew that their father had a filthy temper.

He recalled the day Mr Laird had tried to strike him. It was over something he thought very unimportant; he had just planted a shrub in a place the master had not approved of. Instead of explaining it was not where he wanted it to be, he flew into a rage and raised his arm as if to strike the gardener. Jim put up his hand to ward off the blow, knowing he could be dismissed for this gesture alone, but for some reason, Mr Laird dropped his arm and stormed into the house.

Jim wondered why he was offering money. Surely, a man of Mr Laird's standing could find someone in authority to assist him. Someone must be dealing with the railway workers who were causing so much trouble. Luckily, the railway was not coming anywhere near his house, but he had been told the navvies behaved in a disgusting manner, especially when they'd had too much to drink. Jim had never been a drinker, but he could understand that the unrelenting nature of their work and the way they lived from day to day meant they needed to let off steam.

Chapter Five

WITH NO ONE TO keep track of him, Dawkins made good use of his time with the horse, and when he returned to the town, he went into the Chequers, ostensibly to make enquiries, but mainly to have a few tankards and a chat with his friends. He vowed to mention Master Tobias to them in passing, but he thought he'd done enough searching for the day, and old Ember could have a good drink too, though hers would be at the river. If he wasn't wanted tomorrow, he could take steps to cover the areas where the navvies were working.

The building of the new station, goods yards and houses for Tunbridge was well under way, and he had heard the line ahead to Dover was progressing. He thought it strange the way they were building it in sections, from the Brighton line to Tunbridge. Was it Red Hill where it joined the other line? The areas he would have to search were scattered and it would take a long time, but the money beckoned.

* * *

The past weeks had flown by, but after all Thomas had experienced, he had time to contemplate his future. Yank was right, he could no more work amongst the navvies than he could go back home. And the blasting he heard in the distance reminded him of the man who had died in the explosion.

He glanced round Mrs Grimley's kitchen; a rug made of strips of material had been laid out on the stone floor in front of the range. A pot full of meat stock had been left on the floor, and a blackened kettle lay in the hearth, where it would hang on a hook when hot water was needed. The small window beside the front door was curtainless, but an ornament of a lady dressed in blue stood on the sill, and beside it a candle in a metal holder. Aside from the large, wooden table that he and Mrs Grimley were sitting at, the only other furniture in the room were two further mismatching chairs shoved into the corners and a poorly constructed sideboard with a dresser above it. In the small scullery was a sink with a cupboard underneath it, and a smaller cupboard with a mesh door where Mrs Grimley stored her food. Beside it was a pail of water that Thomas had fetched from the well that morning. He had also cleared out the cinders from the grate and disposed of them. This made him think of the maids, who had to do this job every morning and in every room of their large house. Before now, he had given no thought to the work they did.

He pictured the comfortably furnished home he'd left behind; heavy drapes at the windows and doors, and the chair seats covered in damask; a highly polished table with place settings in the dining room. The drawing room and bedrooms all furnished with the best money could buy. He was happy here in this poor house, but it wasn't the same… He suddenly thought of his brothers and sisters, especially Lizzie. Would their tyrannical father now target her? What could he do for her? He could hardly look after himself.

Mrs Grimley was sewing a patch on one of Yank's undergarments. She glanced up and smiled at him. "You look sad."

"I was thinking of my family." He gave a deep sigh. "Mrs Grimley, can you think of anything I can do? I must earn some money to pay you, otherwise I shall have to find…"

Thomas stopped, realising he would never be able to find anywhere as suitable as where he was now. Yank was so good natured. And how sensible he was in making Thomas realise the position he was in. The boy knew he was thinking of further ways to help him.

"You needn't worry about paying me, young Thomas. I like having you here." She put down her sewing. "We had a son once, Mr Grimley and me, but he died of diphtheria."

"How sad for you. How old was he?"

"Four." Mrs Grimley stared, unseeing, into the distance. "Yes, it was. I lost another child a year later, but we had no more. My husband died six years ago, and that's when I started taking in lodgers."

They shared the silence for a few minutes, and then Thomas said, "Yank is so kind, isn't he?"

"He's one of the very best I've 'ad lodging with me, but I don't suppose it'll be long before he moves on."

Thomas jumped up, clattering the chair as it scraped the stone floor. "Moves on? Where to? Why?"

"Well, dear, the railway work here isn't going to go on forever, is it?" She added, "I suspect Mr Yank will move into Tunbridge or maybe further along the line towards Paddock Wood. Not everything is finished between here and the line that goes to London, Yank told me. I shall miss him terribly."

This devastating news made Thomas feel sick. What would he do now? He looked at Mrs Grimley, his eyes filling with tears, and rushed up to the bedroom.

Later, with Yank back from work, the three of them ate together in silence. Yank, primed by his landlady, sat moodily. Thomas glanced at him every few minutes and sniffed, and Mrs Grimley snapped at them both. That evening, for the first time since Thomas had arrived, Yank went out.

* * *

"Hello, Yank. Not seen you lately. Missed me?" Molly asked hopefully.

"Yes," replied Yank, his voice less than enthusiastic.

"Something's on your mind. Come on, let's go up and you can tell me all about it."

Yank followed her to the attic of the cottage off Bridge Street. The room was cold and damp and the smell from the open ditch outside was unpleasant, to say the least. Molly began to undress, but Yank stopped her. "No, not yet. I want to talk to you."

With a shrug, she put a shawl around her bare shoulders and stepped out of her skirt, leaving it on the floor. Yank strode to the unmade bed and sat down. She joined him. "It's about this boy called Thomas…"

Half an hour later, as they lay side by side, Yank said, "So, what do you think I should do, Molly? I sure don't want him to go back home if he's going to be treated like that again. You should've seen what was done to him." Yank shuddered. "I'm surprised the boy had enough strength to leave and walk for miles till I found him."

Molly had no suggestions. She put her arm across

Yank's chest and kissed him. "You said you've got to move soon. Where are you going? Will you still be able to see me?"

She was not unsympathetic to the plight of the boy, but as she had no answer, she was more interested in Yank and his whereabouts. He was one of her nicer men.

* * *

Thomas sat up when Yank came into the bedroom. The light from the flickering candle illuminated the room.

"Where've you been? I want to talk to you about—"

"Fornicating," Yank said sharply, taking off his jacket, boots and trousers and getting into bed.

"I already told you I don't know what that means."

"Having sex with someone who isn't married to you," Yank snapped.

"I don't know what that means, either. Anyway, I want to know what to do. Mrs Grimley says you're going to move somewhere else. You never told me. What shall I do? Mrs Grimley says I can stay with her, but I don't want to be without you." He burst into tears.

It was half past one, and after his walk to and from Tunbridge, Yank was extremely tired. "Oh, do be quiet. I don't know what you'll do. Go to sleep and we'll talk about it tomorrow... today... in the morning."

Thomas went on crying, now more distressed by Yank's attitude than about his predicament.

Yank blew out the candle. "Stop snivelling, for heaven's sake."

Dawkins was becoming bored with hunting for Tobias. He had been searching for what seemed like weeks. Whilst his theory about the boy being with people no one would expect him to be with was a good one, the railway navvies were seemingly working, or camping, on every plot of land available. There were hundreds of areas where the boy could be, from Tunbridge back to the branch off, and even as far as Staplehurst in the other direction. Not that he thought Tobias would have gone that far.

As he couldn't have the horse that often, his search had to be spread out over several weeks. The lure of the extra coins was not quite as attractive as it had once been.

He was in a beer house in Hildenborough on his way to try his luck north of the town when he got talking to a travelling entertainer. "He's a bit of a novelty, ain't he?" he said, pointing to the monkey on the man's shoulder.

"Yes, always causes interest, especially with the

children. None of 'em ain't ever seen one. Young lad I saw in the village back there was very taken." The man pointed his thumb over his shoulder. "Kept asking questions about what he ate, where he slept and where he came from. Strange lad, looked extremely dirty but spoke well."

Dawkins' ears pricked up. "Spoke well, you say? In Leigh, was it? How long ago?"

"Yes, I think it was called Leigh; hundreds of them navvies on a green. At least four or five weeks ago."

"Interesting."

"Why?"

"Oh, nothing. As you say, seems funny to have a boy speak in a nice voice when he looked so scruffy."

* * *

Thomas tried not to be upset by Yank's attitude. He had been in a foul mood before he left for work, and they had not spoken to each other, let alone discussed anything.

It was boring at the cottage; he had no books and there were no newspapers. He even missed his taciturn tutor. Though Mrs Grimley was kind to him, she was not intelligent, and he couldn't hold a decent conversation with her. He was also getting fed up with the monotony of the provided meals, which comprised endless stews with tough, gristly meat and the same old vegetables, mainly potatoes, carrots and turnips. But he was not in a position to complain. He had brought all this on himself. Mrs Grimley wasn't his mother and Yank wasn't his father. No matter how devoutly he wished they were related, they bore no responsibility for him at all. Thomas helped where he could, but apart from bringing in water from the well, fetching logs to put in the basket beside the range, periodically stoking the fire and cleaning out the ashes, the hours hung heavily. His throat hurt as he tried to hold back his tears. He'd thought he was so grown-up, so sensible he could cope with anything. How foolish, how stupid! The one thing he had learned was how little he knew about the outside world.

He crossed to the window, resting his arms on the sill. Carts and wagons were passing by, as they did day after day, bringing more materials for the railway; fencing posts, sleepers, wood and mysterious metal items he couldn't think of a use for. The Medway Navigation Company brought them up the Medway from Rochester to the wharf in Tunbridge.

Whenever he was in the town, Thomas liked to watch the loading and unloading at the wharf. He and his family had sometimes gone there on market day, but his father hated the noise and the crowded roads and side streets, not to mention the "disgusting people" who inhabited the town. What would he say if he could see his son now?

Thomas blinked. That horse going past looked just

like Ember – it was Ember! And that was Dawkins on him! He ducked down until they were out of sight. So, his father had sent the groom to look for him. He would have to move, or Yank and Mrs Grimley would be in trouble.

Chapter Six

"HE'S GONE, Mr Yank. He's taken all his clothes, I checked – not that he 'ad much – and he even left some coppers on the table."

"When did he go?"

"Don't know exactly. He did the things he usually does for me in the morning. I went to the shops near The Green and when I came back, he'd gone." Mrs Grimley stood disconsolate, her hands in the pockets of her apron. Yank frowned guiltily.

The nights had drawn in and it was dark, wet and cold outside. Where on earth would he go? Surely, he wouldn't try to join the navvy boys. Yank paced up and down the flagstone floor, his boots clattering. He should not have been so harsh. It was not the boy's fault he had been brought up in a wealthy home. Thomas could no more help his circumstances than the men Yank worked with could help theirs.

"Are you going to look for him?" Mrs Grimley looked at him hopefully.

"I don't think there's much point tonight." He thought for a moment. "I could have a quick look around The Green, I suppose." Yank was reluctant to go far on such a night.

"You don't think he's joined them filthy families, do you?"

"I sincerely hope not, ma'am, but you never know. Where would he go and what made him leave so suddenly? Are you sure he didn't say something to you before you left?"

She shook her head. "He's been very sad."

Yank knew why, and that he was responsible for him leaving.

"Well, you could go and have a quick look," Mrs Grimley said, as she put Yank's meal in front of him. "Someone might have noticed him. He does stand out rather."

Exhausted and dispirited though he was, Yank quickly finished his meal and walked along the pitch-dark road past the church and into Leigh. It was ten o'clock, but The Green was a seething mass. There were children playing in the mud, women trying with difficulty to wash clothes. There was even a fight going on in the distance, with men gathered round cheering. Yank thought they probably didn't care who won. It was just a relief from their endless toil. A group of navvies were having a meal served to them in one of the larger makeshift huts that slept fifteen to twenty men. They would often pool their resources to pay a woman to 'keep house' for them. Some other men were staggering back from the beer houses. Yank spoke to one or two he recognised, but they hadn't seen anyone resembling Thomas's description. He retraced his steps back to the cottage, even more worried than he had been the previous night. Thomas might even have decided to go back home, which, while solving his own problems, was not something Yank wanted for the boy. Partly to keep his landlady from nagging him and partly because he also wanted to know Thomas's whereabouts, he told Mrs Grimley that he would try to find out where Thomas lived and if he had returned. He knew the house was near a windmill in Tunbridge, but that wasn't much help. There was more than one mill in the area.

The following day, Yank had a rare morning off, as they were waiting on a delivery of bricks. He walked along Stocks Green Road and through Hildenborough. Just past Hilden House, he thought he saw, to his left, the tips of a mill's sails on rising ground. A gateway bordered a stream beside some fields, where gypsies were stripping and picking hops. It led uphill and into woods, emerging onto a main highway. Yank followed it and was amazed to find himself practically beside the mill itself. A fingerpost indicated that Shipbourne was to the left and Tunbridge was to the right. He wondered if this Shipbourne was the Shibburn that Thomas had mentioned. Why the English did not spell and pronounce words normally he could never understand.

He surveyed the area. There were several wagons waiting by the toll gate. Most were loaded with items for the railway. He hailed a man with a hand cart piled high with vegetables, awaiting his turn to go into town. "Can you tell me if there's a household round here where there are seven children? They are comfortably off."

The man grinned. "Nearly everybody in this part of the town is comfortably off, and most people have large families. Down there—" he indicated a crossroad ahead "—to the left, there's a double-fronted house; they've got six kids at least, possibly more. I deliver there sometimes."

Yank hurried along the road, turned left and stood outside the house the man had described, trusting it was Thomas's. Should he knock on the front door? What would he say? Perhaps the servants' entrance would be better; they were less likely to become hysterical if Thomas hadn't returned. He went down the side of the building. In the distance, a gardener was working. Mr Jim, from London, no doubt. Yank knocked on the green wooden door with his knuckles. It was opened by a slim, pasty-faced girl.

"I'm sorry to trouble you, but could I speak to someone in charge?"

She stood gaping at him.

"Who is it, Tilda?" A voice called.

"It's a man, Cook. He speaks funny." Tilda's mouth fell back open.

Cook bustled to the door. "Tilda, don't be so rude." She barged the girl out of the way and addressed Yank. "How can I help you?"

The woman looked Yank up and down, no doubt wondering what this man could possibly want.

"Well, ma'am, I heard that someone in the household had disappeared, and I wondered if that person had returned."

"Do you know anything about Tobias? Master will be pleased."

"Well, no." Yank quickly had to think what to say without giving anything away.

"Come in. You look a bit weary. Perhaps I can offer you a cordial?"

Yank would have preferred ale, but he replied, "That's mighty kind of you, ma'am, thank you."

At least he might glean some information about Thomas, well, Tobias, it seemed.

"Sit down there."

Tilda, still gawping, was told to get some cordial

from the pantry and then get on with cleaning the pans.

"So, how do you know about Master Tobias going missing?"

"News gets around." Yank did not expand, the less she knew about him the better.

Tilda put an earthenware cup, filled to the brim, in front of Yank. Some of the contents slopped on the table. Cook slapped her hand. "Be more careful, girl. Go and get some carrots and potatoes for tonight's meal. Leave the pans for now. The gardener's out there, he'll tell you what you can have."

Reluctantly, the kitchen maid picked up a basket and slowly made for the kitchen door. Yank was sure she would much rather clean the pans and listen to what they had to say.

"Now, where was I? Oh, yes, Master Tobias. He's been gone some weeks, and nothing seen nor heard of 'im. Very strange it is. Mrs Laird and Miss Elizabeth are very upset."

"Yes, I'm sure."

Surprisingly, nothing was said of Mr Laird's emotions. Yank figured Miss Elizabeth must be the 'Lizzie' Thomas had mentioned.

"What made him leave? Was it sudden?"

"Well." She lowered her voice. "We think his father beat him. Mind you, he was always chastising the children, 'cept the baby, of course, though I wouldn't put that past him..."

"I see," Yank said. He drained his drink and, rising from his chair, said, "I'll make a point of looking out for him. What does he look like?"

Cook gave what Yank thought was an excellent description of Thomas. "If you hear of anything, tell me," she said. "There's a reward, you know."

"I'll bear that in mind, Cook."

She beamed at the familiarity and Yank beamed back. "What sort of things is the young man interested in? Do you think he might have gone to London to seek his fortune? You know what young people are like nowadays." He raised his shoulders and grinned.

"Wouldn't think he had any money to get there. He's keen on the new railway coming to Tunbridge, I do know that – always talking about it."

"Is that so? Well, now I know exactly what he looks like, I shall be able to keep my eyes open for him." He crossed to the kitchen door. "Thank you for the drink, ma'am."

In his effort not to give too much of himself away, he had forgotten to disguise his accent. Not much point in worrying about that now. Just as well the cook had not been more curious and inquisitive about this strange visit.

Yank began his long walk back to Leigh – a weary two hours at least.

* * *

Thomas tried hard to think what he should do. Money was the problem. He only had three shillings left. While three or four pence would possibly get him a bed for the night at some sort of hostelry, he didn't want to go to a place where he would be noticed. As Yank had persuaded him that working on the railway was out of the question, the only other job he could think of was hop or fruit picking. He was sure he could manage that without too much trouble.

Instead of going towards Tunbridge, he decided it would be better to make his way along the railway track towards Penshurst. The family had passed through the village in their carriage on their way to his parents' friends, but they had never stopped there. He would try his luck in that direction.

He kept as close to the track as he could without getting in the way of the navvies or their work. Periodically, he stood staring, spellbound by the enormity of the planning and design, not to mention the hard labour. He had learned from Yank that the railway was not being built directly from the Brighton line to Dover, as he had once thought, but in sections, simultaneously. Now he came to think of it, he had read about a big accident in Dover, when five men were killed while excavating the tunnels and demolishing cliffs, so he should have gathered how it was being constructed, and Yank had mentioned what was going on past Tunbridge. Thomas wondered how Yank knew so much about what was happening so far away. He never saw him with a newspaper. His father took the *Maidstone Journal* and *The Times*, which he read avidly when his father had finished with them.

It was only about two miles from Leigh to Penshurst, but Thomas was tired. The ground was muddy, making walking slower, and the scenery was dreary, as the hop fields were almost denuded, and poles stood stark like rows of tall, thin soldiers. Most farms specialised in hops, but here and there were some fruit trees, which the farmers used to bring in money after their hops had finished. Other farms specialised exclusively in fruit.

It was dusk and he had to find somewhere to sleep, even if that was out in the open. He had reached the new Penshurst Station, which Yank had said he'd had a hand in building.

From the roadside, Thomas saw gypsies preparing to leave the hop field. His father didn't approve of them; Thomas didn't know why, but then his father didn't seem to approve of much in the world.

"Does the owner want any more pickers, do you know?" he asked an olive-skinned woman wearing a black shirt covered by a shawl and a long black skirt. From her ears hung round gold hoops. Thomas thought how attractive she was. Before the young woman could answer, a man came over and asked what he wanted, and she drifted away.

"I wondered if I could do some picking, though it looks as if you've nearly finished."

"Yes, we're packing up now and going back to our camp, then we will pick apples or some other crop on our way back to London."

"I don't mean now, I mean tomorrow, or some time."

"Have you done this work before?"

"No, but I wouldn't think it was that difficult. I could watch you."

The man gave a wry grin. "The owner is Mr Acott, and he lives in that house up the road." He pointed to a two-storey building at the crossroad. "He might take you on for the last day or two, but you gets paid by how much you picks – so much a basket." He pointed to a large wicker basket nearby. "When that's filled you get thruppence."

Thomas stared at the basket and thought how it would take ages to fill, but he pulled back his shoulders and said to himself he had no option if he wanted money. "Thank you. I'll go and see him now."

The gypsy looked him up and down and liked what he saw, even though he was not one of them. Nice voice, too.

Tentatively, Thomas knocked on the farm door. The woman who answered asked what he wanted. Remembering to put on a less educated voice, he said, "Can I do some picking?" He wondered whether he should have added "ma'am" like Yank did.

She frowned. "I'll ask my husband, it's doubtful,

65

we're nearly finished." She turned away and called, "Young man here wants to know if he can pick."

Mrs Acott, for that was who Thomas assumed she was, left him on the doorstep.

Mr Acott duly appeared. "Only a day or so to go. Where've you come from?"

Thomas was not expecting this question. Flustered, he said, "I've come from Lunnun. I come dahn last week to see… um… me uncle, but he'd gorn away and I ain't got no money to get 'ome."

"I see. Well, come back in the morning and—"

"'Ave you got anywhere I can sleep tonight?"

"There are a couple of huts some hop pickers use, mostly they live in tents. Nearly all of them have gone now, but one or two of the Irish travellers are still around." He pointed the way Thomas had just come. "The huts are just before Whitepost Farm. You can stay in one of those two."

Thomas had had nothing to eat since breakfast at Mrs Grimley's. He'd walked for what seemed like miles and his legs felt so weak he could hardly put one foot in front of the other. He pushed open the door of the first of the huts. Penshurst Place itself could not have been more welcoming to him, he said to himself, as he fell on the bare bed.

Thomas was in a deep sleep when suddenly he roused. A noise had woken him. He lay still and listened. Someone was in his hut. What should he do? Pretend to be asleep? Challenge the person? He

66

opened his eyes but could see little. Slowly, he raised his head. Someone was going through his coat pocket – he had left his money in there. What a stupid fool he was. Hadn't Yank warned him about thieves?

Could he challenge the intruder? If nothing else, he had learned that he was not as robust as he thought he was. Instead, he pretended to stir in his sleep and rolled over. The man – he assumed it to be a man – hurried out of the hut, not worrying about banging the door as he hastily left.

Thomas got up and searched his coat. All his money had gone.

Chapter Seven

TILDA WASN'T sure what to do. Miss Elizabeth had told her to say if she heard anything about Master Tobias, but she wasn't sure she had. Cook had sent her out into the garden before she could gather anything useful, but she did hear the man asking if anyone had returned. He could only be talking about Tobias. Then she saw Miss Elizabeth walking in the garden and slipped out before Cook, who had left to discuss the day's meals with Mrs Laird, would be back to stop her.

"I think I might 'ave some news, Miss. There was a man came 'ere yesterday. I think dat he knew something 'bout Master Tobias."

Lizzie's eyes lit up, and she grabbed Tilda by her shoulders. "What did he say? Did he mention my brother?"

"I didn't hear nuffin much, 'cause Cook sent me to

get a drink for him, and then I 'ad to go into the garden to pick—"

"Yes, yes," Lizzie said, still grasping Tilda's shoulders, "but you must have heard something. Think, girl, think. Tell me exactly what happened."

"Well, I answered the door."

"Which door, the front?"

"Oh, no, Miss. I ain't allowed upstairs or in the hall less it's somefin' special."

"Well, go on."

"He had a funny voice. Didn't come from round 'ere, and 'e didn't sound like the gardener."

"What did he say?"

"I can't remember all the words, something like 'e knew dat someone was missing and 'ad they come back."

"Anything else?"

Tilda's brows drew together. "Cook asked how he 'ad 'eard 'bout Master Tobias."

"Yes, yes, go on."

"And I think he said 'news gets round', or somefin like dat. Then Cook sent me out into the garden. 'Ave I done the right thing? I don't want to get into no trouble." She twisted one hand with the other, afraid she would get into bother with Cook if she were found out.

"Thank you, Tilda, you've done very well. I will give you something later."

As the girl turned to leave, Lizzie asked, "What do you mean by a funny voice?"

"I don't know, I ain't never 'eard anyone speak like dat."

Elizabeth frowned. "All right, Tilda, you can go."

What could the girl mean? she pondered as she went through the French doors into the house. And why would someone come to see if Tobias had returned? Not unless he knew he was missing in the first place. "News gets round" was not exactly an explanation for a visit. She sat down. Who could she confide in? She clamped her bottom lip between her teeth. At least Tobias wasn't dead and was, presumably, still in the area. But where? Oh, how she wished she were a man and could go searching for him herself. At that moment, she caught a glimpse of Mr Jim at the bottom of the garden. She brightened. He might be able to suggest what a 'funny voice' could mean. With that, she jumped up and returned to the garden.

Yank was bidding Mrs Grimley farewell. He had found himself lodgings in Tunbridge and had been delegated to work in the town itself, either on the houses being built for railway workers near the new station, or on the bridge. He had been told that Mr Cubitt, the main contractor, had thought about the railway going over a lowered road, but that would have been more expensive. So, with some negotiating with the Turnpike Trust, it had been decided that the road would go over the railway. There was a great deal of bricklaying work in that area, so it was sensible to find lodgings close by.

"I shall miss you, Mr Yank," Mrs Grimley remarked, putting a dirty cotton rag to her eyes. "What with Thomas going as well, I shall be so lonely. What shall I do if he comes back? Will you leave me an address so I can tell you if he does?"

"By all means, Mrs Grimley." He wrote down an address in Barden Road. He didn't think she could read very well, if at all, but she could always get someone else to contact him. "But, somehow, I don't think he will come back. I'm very sorry about it. We tried hard, didn't we, ma'am?" *But not hard enough*, Yank thought to himself. "I guess it's for the best. He may go home, eventually."

"To that dreadful father. I hope not."

"But living like we do isn't what he's used to. I don't think he'd manage."

"No, I don't think so, either." She sniffed. "He was such a nice lad."

"If someone does come enquiring, don't give too much away. We could still be in trouble."

"Oh, I can be quite canny when I want to be, Mr Yank. I'll mind what I say."

* * *

"Mr Jim."

He stopped digging and rested on his spade. "Yes, Miss Elizabeth?"

"Tilda, our kitchen maid, told me someone had come to the house saying he'd heard a person was missing and asking if he'd returned. Don't you think that strange?"

"Yes, Miss, I certainly do." He frowned. "There must be some connection."

"The other clue is—" Lizzie spoke excitedly "—Tilda said he sounded funny. Trouble is, she can't explain what she means; just said it wasn't like you speak, or like the people around here. Have you any ideas?"

He resumed his puzzled look. "No, Miss Elizabeth, I can't say I do. Could she mean he was a foreigner, from France perhaps?"

"Yes, he could be." She paused; her brows furrowed. "But if he had that strong an accent, I don't think Tilda would have understood him at all."

Mr Jim pushed back his battered leather hat and scratched his head. "I can't think what she meant. What about asking Cook?"

Lizzie didn't want to involve Cook, who would go telling tales to Father. In fact, she probably had already; she liked to keep on the right side of him. Not that she could blame her.

Lizzie's silence made Mr Jim think along the same lines. "'Ere, Miss. I've just 'ad a thought. Perhaps he was Irish, or a Scotch man. They'd all be speaking English, wouldn't they?"

"Oh, Mr Jim, you are clever. I bet that's it. Now, what can I do about it?"

"You can't do nothing, and don't you try," he admonished. "But tell you what, I'll ask around. This man more than likely works on the new railway."

"On the other hand, Mr Jim," Lizzie said, "I know Tilda's a bit simple, but I think she would recognise a Scot or Irishman. Who else speaks English?"

Mr Jim stared into the distance. How he wanted to help Lizzie. "There are men from the north who worked on railways up there, I was told; they would be hard to understand." Suddenly inspired, he added, "What about an American? Railway building is going on in nearly every country, I believe."

"Yes!" Her brow creased. "Though I don't know I've ever heard about Americans in this area, but it's something we could think about. And now you come to mention the railway, Tobias was always talking about it and couldn't wait for it to come to the town. Please, Mr Jim, do see if you can get some news of him."

Tears welled in her eyes, and seeing her so upset, poor Mr Jim was almost brought to tears himself.

The truth was that Jim Redman did not want to get involved at all. He told his wife all the information he had gleaned, and she agreed. The trouble was, he had such a soft spot for the girl – and for that matter, for Master Tobias, too – that he would do anything to help. Mr Laird, he gathered, had offered a reward for news, but Jim wasn't interested in any financial gain, welcome as it would be. He had three children, and another on the way, so money wasn't plentiful. However, the thought of helping Mr Laird to get his son back only to beat him again was not one he could reconcile with. Miss Elizabeth, on the other hand, needed to know where her brother was, and if he was safe.

That evening, he went out to the Chequers. He considered it about the most central of the inns and beer houses in the town, along with the Rose & Crown, which was a bit too pricey for him. He met a couple of acquaintances and asked if they knew of a man with an accent, not mentioning which one. They shook their heads. There were only a few people at the tables, and he went over to the two who looked the least objectionable. They appeared the better dressed, too.

"Working with anyone who doesn't speak like us?"

"Why you askin'?" one of them asked. He sounded suspicious.

Flustered at the question, Jim said, "I heard there was… there was, er, an American amongst the navvies. My wife has a relative who went to America, and she wondered what life was like there, and if he knew him."

The men guffawed. "America's a big place. How would anyone know about her relative?"

Jim reddened. It was a stupid explanation. "Well, I just wondered."

He turned away, but one of the men said, "We don't know anyone working as a navvy, but there's a bricklayer called Big Yank. Don't know him, mind; just heard about him." He turned to his friend. "Do you know him?"

His friend shook his head. "No, but judging by the name…"

"Yes, yes, that sounds like it. Thank you. My wife will be pleased. Have you any idea where I might find him?"

"None at all, we work all over the place. Try another beer house at the other end of town, where the station will be. There'll be a lot of building going on there, as they hope to open to Tunbridge in early '42. This chap you're wanting could be involved there. We're both moving with our contractor further down the line next week, past Staplehurst."

"Well, thank you for your help. I'll tell the wife and we might make a trip down that end of the town one evening."

"Rather you than me. If I were you, I wouldn't make it a Friday or Saturday night."

75

* * *

Yank was at Molly's. With Thomas off his hands and being closer to her lodging house, he could see her more often.

He was staring up at the peeling plasterwork between the beams. What he would like, he considered, was a small place of his own somewhere in Kent. This county seemed a mighty fine place to live. The railway was going to bring people into the countryside, and that meant more houses, which, in turn, meant more work for him. He might even stay in Tunbridge. He guessed there would have to be more houses built for the railway workers, and he had heard talk of farmland that might be sold in the future, especially if the railway brought more business to the town. People could even go up to London to work and come back the same day. What a wonderful thing that would be.

Reluctantly, his thoughts turned to Thomas, who he couldn't shake from his mind. Where could he have gone? Had anyone taken him under their wing? The boy wasn't used to fending for himself, and he was too… too cultured – was that the word? – to be wandering around seeking work.

"What yer thinking 'bout now?" Molly asked impatiently. "Not that kid again?"

"Yeah."

"There ain't a lot you can do 'bout it, is there?"

"No, I know, but I can't help it. He sure led a very sheltered life."

"He'll 'ave to manage, like we all 'ave to. Poor little rich boy."

"I told you before, he can't help being born rich any more than we can help being poor."

"My 'eart bleeds for 'im."

"Anyway, his father nearly beat him to a pulp. Rich or not, no one deserves that."

"Plenty of kids get beaten."

"Oh, do be quiet, Molly."

"That's nice, I must say. So, wot yer going to do?"

"Dunno. Nothing, I guess."

Jim Redman thought it better that his wife didn't come with him when he made his trip to the south of the town. He rarely had reason to go that way, as there were few houses to speak of and, more often than not, that area flooded. The smell was none too pleasant either. All his gardening work was to the north of the town and towards Shipbourne. It was quite dark when he reached The Angel Hotel. His boots squelched as he walked, and he was appalled at the state of the road. There was so much churned up mud from where wagons and carts carrying materials for the railway, not to mention the heavy stuff from the Medway Navigation Company at the wharf, constantly moved up and down Bridge Street. Crowds of people milled about, either curious, excited or appalled by the work going on around them. Jim didn't know where to start searching or who to ask. What did the chap in the Chequers call the man? Something Yank? Tall Yank? No, Big Yank, that was it. Probably because he was tall and well built.

Who could he approach? It seemed the workers were finishing their shifts, as they were moving en masse to the nearest hostelry. Every man looked as if he would knock you down as soon as speak to you. Their clothes were disgustingly stiff with mud. He plucked up some courage and hailed three men. "Excuse me," he said.

They strode straight past him, almost knocking him off his feet in the process. He felt like a foreigner in his own country.

The next man was on his own. Perhaps he would have a better chance with him. "Excuse me," he said again, standing in front of him and hoping he would not be trampled to death.

"Yeah?"

"Do you know a man called Big Yank?"

"Yeah, I 'eard of him."

"Good." Jim sighed with relief. "Could you tell me where I can find him?"

"No, can't." He barged past too.

Jim's shoulders slumped. At least there *was* a man

called Big Yank. He would try one more time and then he would give up. He couldn't wait to get home.

Boldly, he said to the next two men coming his way, "Big Yank, do you know him?"

"Yeah, recently moved this way – don't know where, though. Stick around a while and you might meet someone who does."

Jim didn't fancy sticking around, but if he were to help Miss Elizabeth, at least with some information, he would have to try harder. He had now reached the area where the railway met the turnpike. What a difference it would make to the town – to everyone! He had never really thought deeply about the changes it would bring. His wife's cousin, who was a sheep farmer on Romney Marsh, had explained last time they saw him that if the railway came near him, he would be able to send his sheep up to London by train instead of having to drive them to Smithfield. That alone would be a big saving. The sheep lost a lot of weight over the four days the drive took, and a few of them even died on the journey.

While Jim hovered, searching for someone who looked likely to help without injuring him, he thought about the future. Perhaps he could go up to London, take the wife and kids, show them where he had lived as a boy. Well, he could if he could afford it. He had no idea what it would cost, but what an adventure. They might even see the new queen.

Some men in the distance looked as if they were

fencing the two tracks going towards Paddock Wood. Jim supposed the line might be nearing Ashford by now. He glanced to where the Priory ruins used to be; building work was happening at speed for what he assumed was the new station. How everything was changing! After standing for a while, he remembered he was supposed to be looking for Big Yank. There seemed to be enough men milling around there; surely someone would know where this man could be found, especially if he was a large man, as his name suggested.

He tackled a man not quite as filthy as the navvies he had previously encountered, though he was covered in brick dust from head to toe. "Do you know an American by the name of—?"

"Oh, you mean Big Yank. He was here a minute ago. Still got some bricking to finish before he quits. Go over there—" he pointed a dirty finger "—behind where they're starting the station foundations; he'll be working on the new houses. See? Cracking on apace they are. He'll be there somewhere."

"Thank you, thank you very much." Jim could not believe his luck.

Chapter Eight

THOMAS STAGGERED from his hut the next morning weak with hunger and fatigue.

After the theft, he had spent the rest of the night crying. He thought of his mother and Lizzie, and of Yank. Why had Yank deserted him? Should he go home? Should he try to trace Yank and see if he had any new ideas about how to earn some money?

He needed to change his clothes. Although by now they were as filthy as a navvy's, they still showed their quality and were a giveaway to all who met him. Could Mrs Grimley help him? But Dawkins might be lurking there.

He was afraid of every aspect of his life now; the people he met; not knowing what to say; having to remember his speech and the words he used. Though he considered himself strong, he was not accustomed to hours of backbreaking work and having to live on his wits.

"Bad night?" a man asked, as he passed him at the midday break, a sly grin on his face.

"Yes. Someone stole some money of mine." Thomas stared hungrily at the bread and cheese the man was eating.

"Too bad. You should take more care." He laughed, and Thomas was sure he was the culprit.

He worked hard to fill his basket, but he was slow. He had not quite reached the brim. He waited until everyone else had been paid and he was the only one left, but, as he held out his hand, he fell at Mr Acott's feet in a dead faint.

* * *

Today, the reward had renewed its pull over Dawkins. He had not had the horse for some time, so it was with fresh anticipation that he was riding along the Stocks Green Road to Leigh, hoping to glean some information on this boy with the educated voice. His first stop was the shop, which was the best place to collect rumour and gossip. However, all he was regaled with was complaints about the navvies and their fighting, drinking, foul language, damage to property and theft.

One man was incensed that after all he'd had to put up with, there wasn't even going to be a station at

Leigh. "It's all right for Penshurst and South Park, they're important," he grumbled. "I bet they don't put up with what we've had to put up with." There were nods of agreement all round.

When Dawkins, who'd wisely nodded along to everything that was being said, asked about a lost boy, no one was able to come up with anything helpful. Dismayed, he went out into the fetid air. Skirting The Green, he chanced upon a navvy sitting in front of a crudely constructed hut. He had a gash to his face and dried blood clung to the wound and down his cheek. Though he was a burly man, his face was grey with pain. Dawkins wasn't sure whether to speak to him. From what he had gathered in the shop, you took your life in your hands if you so much as glanced their way.

"Have you seen a boy round these parts recently?" he asked. "He's dressed in nice clothes, and he could be looking for a job on the railway."

"If 'e were wearing nice clothes, 'e's 'ardly likely to be wanting work 'ere, now, is he?" The man winced and, raising his hand to his head, gave a cry of pain.

"You ought to get that wound attended to," said Dawkins.

"Ain't no doctor round 'ere who'd be bothered. There was some talk of getting money together to pay one." He laughed. "Nothing's come of it so far."

"So," Dawkins said, "you've not seen a young boy?"

The man stroked his chin and shifted on the muddy ground. "Well, there was a man with a boy who came from London. He was staying with his landlady."

The groom perked up. "Who was that?" Tobias might not come from London, but it would be a different voice from what was usually heard around here – something out of the ordinary, like the hurdy-gurdy man had described. "What did he look like?"

"He was about fifteen or sixteen, five-foot-six or seven."

"What about his clothes?"

"Bit scruffy." He frowned. "Now you come to mention it, the clothes looked quite good."

"Do you know the man he was with?"

"Yeah, the American." The man closed his eyes.

"American!" Dawkins said, surprised. "Where does he live?"

"Don't know. He wasn't a…a… nav…" The man suddenly appeared to lose consciousness and keeled over to one side. Dawkins was tempted to bend down and give the man a shake, but a woman appeared from another ramshackle hut close by. "This man is very ill," he said. "Can you get some help for him?"

With that, he returned to the tethered Ember, gave him an apple he had picked on the way and went back to the shop.

"Can you tell me if an American has been lodging nearby," he asked a woman buying butter.

"I don't know about an American, but there are several cottagers around here that take in lodgers. Cashing in on the situation, you might say. Why don't you try them?"

"Can you give me some addresses?"

Pulling scraps of paper and something to write with from her pockets, the woman supplied the information and Dawkins, whose education was rudimentary, laboriously wrote down as near as he could the places mentioned. "Thank you, you have been a great help," he said.

"Are you... um... Big Yank?" Jim asked timidly, worried about his reception.

"That's what I'm called. Who are you and what d'you want with me?" Suspiciously, Yank looked the man up and down. Neatly dressed, he thought, but poor-quality garments.

Excited at having found his mystery man, Jim rambled on. "It's Miss Elizabeth, yer see, she asked me to find out 'bout Tobias, and I've been asking questions cause I want to find 'im. You see, she's—"

"Just a minute. Who's Miss Elizabeth and who's Tobias?"

Yank already knew the answers to his questions, but he wanted to know what else was going on in the Laird household.

"Oh, they're brother and sister. He's run away and she's worried. I said I would try and find out 'bout him, and so far, it's led to you, but I don't know if I'm on the right track. I just want to do it for Miss Elizabeth. I don't like to see the girl so upset." Jim stared at Yank. He was so different from the picture he'd formed in his mind. He wasn't tall or broad like he had imagined; he was quite wiry of build and of average height. His hair was fair, and his face was brown through working out in the open. Jim sucked in his bottom lip and frowned.

Ah, thought Yank, this must be Mr Jim, the gardener from London, who, according to Thomas, was a nice fellow. How much could he take this man into his confidence? Even more disturbingly, it brought the young man to mind again, just when he had been desperately trying to forget him. How much should he reveal? Just enough for the sister to know that he was alive? Yank was brought back by the gardener asking in a hopeful way if he could help.

"I don't know where he is now, but he was alive and reasonably well a while ago, in Leigh. Is that enough information?"

"Can you tell me more?"

"Yes, but I don't want to. I might get myself and another person into trouble. Do you get my meaning?"

"Yes." Mr Jim nodded his head. "You found 'im and sheltered 'im and now he's gone again. Do ya 'appen to know, I mean, did he tell you, er, why he ran away?"

"Do you know enough about his father to guess?"

Jim nodded knowingly. "Thank you for what you've told me. Let's leave it there, shall we?" He turned to go. "I'm not the only person searching for him, you know?"

"I guess not. He was a great guy. I liked him very much."

Liked, he'd said *liked,* as if Thomas were dead. How Yank's conscience pricked.

John Soper, the Parish Constable, and his assistant, John Carpenter, were concluding the meeting of the Vestry. Soper turned to Carpenter and, taking a piece of paper from his pocket, said, "I have a note here left by the servant of a Mr Laird who lives in the north of the town. "It seems," he added, peering at the writing, "that Mr Laird has requested that we search for his son, who, it seems, has been missing for some time. Strangely, it doesn't say for how long."

"Doesn't he think we have enough to do?" Carpenter moaned. "We haven't got a constabulary like Tunbridge Wells, and we only meet occasionally. Now that the railway is coming, our part-time, mostly unpaid duties seem to have more than doubled."

"Probably doesn't know what we do at all, apart

from trying to keep the navvies off their property and being at their beck and call for a situation such as this." Soper paused and stroked his beard. "I wonder how much influence this Mr Laird has in the town? I don't want to ignore him if he's going to cause us a lot more trouble. I think I'll go up to the house and find out as much as I can."

* * *

"A constable to see you, sir."

The housemaid ushered into the study a tall, thin, bearded man dressed in a neat suit.

Putting on his most affable face, Mr Laird motioned for the man to sit. "You have been told, I assume, that I have a rather delicate matter with which I hope you can help?"

"Yes, sir, we'll do our best."

Mr Laird related the facts of the disappearance of his son, Tobias, and how he'd been visited by a mysterious man asking pertinent questions.

"If this person was wondering if my son had returned," continued Mr Laird, "I must assume he knew he had left here, in which case I would like to speak to him. So, constable, there are two things I want you to do. Seek out this man. If he's an American, as my cook surmises, there cannot many of them around. I expect he works on the railway." He turned up his nose. "Secondly, I would like you to search for my son. Of course, one might lead to the other."

As Mr Laird spoke, Soper began taking notes. He looked up enquiringly. "Can you think of any reason why your son left so suddenly, sir?"

"Why, no." Mr Laird waved his arm in an arc and grinned smugly. "As you can see, he lives a very comfortable life here."

Soper gazed around the room. Fringed heavy curtains at the window, books in a large glass cabinet, a marble fireplace with a coal fire burning brightly and a huge desk with a leather tooled top, behind which Mr Laird was seated.

"How did he leave?" Soper turned a page of his notebook.

"What do you mean?"

"Was it during the day? How did you discover he had gone? What, if anything, did he take with him?"

"One of my sons informed me in the morning that he had left during the night. He took a few clothes with him."

"Did your son see him go?"

"No, he was as surprised as I was – we all were. My wife is most distressed."

"So, you cannot think of anything that might have caused him to take such a drastic step?"

"No, indeed. As I told you, there was no indication that he intended to leave. It is my opinion that he was influenced by some unsavoury characters, some ne'er do wells."

Soper frowned. "How would he come across such people? Is he often out alone?"

Mr Laird coughed. "Well, no."

"You say your son left some time ago. Why didn't you inform the Vestry sooner?"

"I… I… er, hoped he would return."

"Um." Soper felt uneasy. "Had anything happened previously that might have upset him?" he asked. "Or have you since heard something that might give a clue as to where he would head? Do you think he intended to go to London?"

"If I knew that," Mr Laird said with some asperity, tired of being quizzed by this inferior man, "do you think I would be asking you to look for him? As I told you, the only clue came from my cook. She said a man came to the tradesmen's door and asked if Tobias had returned home, so he must have known that he had disappeared in the first place, don't you think?"

"Yes, it would seem so. Did he call your son by name?"

Mr Laird frowned. "I don't think so. I surmise, from what my cook said, that this man had heard that someone from this house had gone missing."

"What was the man's name?"

"She didn't ask, but she thought from the way he spoke that he might be an American, as I already told you. She didn't think he was from around this part of Kent, anyway."

Soper continued to scribble in his notebook. That was a big help. He had been thinking this mystery man might have been Irish, or from the north of England. He suspected the pompous Mr Laird was hiding something, and he believed it strange that he had waited so long before asking for help. Was he really awaiting his son's return?

"As you know, with the railway coming, the noise and disruption it causes and the trouble we have with the navvies, our resources are very stretched," he explained. "The excavators and everybody to do with the railway are everywhere. Now, sir, perhaps you could give me a few further details about your son's disappearance and I will get back to you."

Chapter Nine

THOMAS CAME to on a chair in the kitchen of the Acotts' farmhouse. Mrs Acott had her arm round him.

"You fainted, young man. My husband brought you in here. You've not had anything to eat for some time, have you?"

Thomas shook his head. "I had three shillings, but I couldn't find anywhere to stay, and now that money has been stolen, so I only have what you've just given me. Can I buy something to eat from you?"

"There's no need to give me money, I'll get you some pie and a drink of milk. How come you are in such a state? Have you run away from home?"

Mrs Acott was neatly dressed in a white blouse, a thick brown wool skirt and an apron which, Thomas thought, was beautifully white, just like Cook's, though not like Mrs Grimley's. She busied herself round the farmhouse kitchen opening cupboards and preparing food. A baby fast asleep in a cradle to the side of the inglenook reminded him of Charlotte, and the young children he could hear playing in the dusk outside the window brought to mind his other siblings. A lump came to his throat.

"Yes," Thomas replied, quickly wiping a tear from his eye. He had not intended to admit he was a runaway, but he decided there was no use pretending otherwise.

"I can see you are not from a poor background."

"No."

"What made you do such a thing?"

She told him to pull his chair up to the table and placed the plate and cup before him.

Resisting the temptation to gollop the pie, he took small bites. Food had never tasted so delicious. He ignored Mrs Acott's question and changed the subject. "The money I had would have seen me through until I got some more work. I wanted a job on the new railway, but I'm not strong enough." He took a swig of the milk. "Can you think of something I can do?" He wiped his mouth on the only handkerchief he had with him, which he hastily put away after noticing its colour.

"My husband can't give you work now hop picking and apples are finished, and he has enough labourers for the farm."

Thomas nodded sadly. "How many children have you got, Mrs Acott?"

"Five." She looked over towards the window and smiled. "They're waiting for their father, who'll be in soon. Then we'll all sit down and have our meal."

How lovely to sit around the table together. Thomas was sure they would not be sitting there afraid to speak or comment.

He rose from the chair. "Thank you for looking after me," he said.

Slowly, he walked up the road to his hut. He seemed destined to be on the move like a common criminal – a fugitive, yes, that was the word. He had read it in a novel. Could he live like this for the rest of his life?

* * *

Dawkins had spent nearly all morning trying the addresses he had been given. The last one was on his way home. He would just have to tell Mr Laird that he could do no more. Shame about the money.

He knocked on the cottage door. "Mrs Gimble?"

"No, no one of that name here."

He peered at his piece of paper and tried to read his writing. "Perhaps it's Grimble?"

She shook her head.

Dawkins was sure he had the right address if not the name. "So, what is your name, then?" he barked.

Mrs Grimley did not like his tone. "Why're you asking?"

"Because I have been told you take in lodgers from the railway."

"Oh, you want a room, then? Why didn't you say so in the first place?"

"No, I'm looking for a lost boy."

Mrs Grimley was immediately on her guard. "A lost boy! Where has he escaped from? The workhouse?"

"No, no, he's the son of my employer."

"A bit careless of someone. What's his name, then?"

"Tobias. Tobias Laird."

"Never heard of him."

"I've been told that a boy from London stayed with you a few weeks ago."

"Now, who told you that? Bet you've been in that shop. Nosey lot. Anyway, he's gone back. He was a relative of me husband."

Dawkins' shoulders slumped. That was not going to get him a reward. He turned away and unhitched Ember.

"What's your name?" he called as she went to shut the door.

"Grimley. Margery Grimley. Sorry I can't 'elp you."

As she turned into her kitchen, she muttered under her breath, "Glad I couldn't help; don't like the look of you. Perhaps I'd better send a message to Mr Yank."

* * *

Thomas was quite certain he knew who had taken his money. His name was Charlie, and when Thomas overheard him making plans to go drinking with a fellow picker, he hatched a plan to retrieve his money.

That evening, he hid behind some chestnut hop poles that were leaning against a wall near the huts and waited until Charlie came back with his friend, who cheerily bid him goodnight before making his way to his own lodgings.

After waiting a while, until he was sure Charlie would have fallen asleep, he stood up and stretched. He then crept up to Charlie's hut and listened for a while. The man's breathing was heavy and interspersed with one or two grunts and snores. Thomas was trembling, and his knees felt as if they would buckle any minute, but he was unwavering in his resolve. As he slowly lifted the metal latch and pushed the door open a smidge, he saw Charlie turn over. He held his breath, poised to run for his life if he needed to.

The snoring continued. He peered into the room, but it was dark, and he could barely see the bed, let alone anything else. Charlie kept his personal effects in the pockets of his coat, which he'd probably hung on a hook behind the door. Thomas cautiously stepped inside the hut, all the while keeping his eyes fixed on the bed. Still no movement. He turned around so he was facing the door and felt for the coat. Reaching into one of the pockets, he felt only a piece of cloth. In another was a tin of something, tobacco probably, and some matches, but no money. Charlie turned over in his bed once again, and Thomas stiffened with fright. Would the cold air from the open door rouse him? He stood rigid, his heart beating so fast and loudly that he was sure it would wake Charlie if the breeze didn't. When he had settled, Thomas searched an inside pocket. At last, he found what he was searching for. He had to feel how much was there. Two sixpences, some copper coins – farthings and pennies – four shillings and, he thought, half a crown. Thomas extracted his three shillings, resisting the temptation to take more, and quickly left.

As he got into bed in the hut next door, he couldn't stop laughing. He had never been so frightened or so elated. He knew Yank thought he was too genteel to live on his wits, but he would have been proud of him tonight. With the little money he had earned, plus his three shillings, he *would* make his way in the world, and he *would* find work with something to do with the railway, no matter what Yank thought.

Chapter Ten

"HELLO, John. What did you find out?" asked Carpenter.

"It seems an American is a key factor in the boy's disappearance," replied Soper.

"That should make things easier."

"Yes, but I'm not sure where to start. There's building work going on all over the place, especially around the station."

"Why not start there, then. Just ask for an American. I'm sure there can't be many of them in Tunbridge."

"Good thinking. I'll go there tomorrow morning."

"By the way, I've had a report of poaching on Mr Alexander's land. Perhaps you could look into that while you're in the area."

* * *

John Soper stood near the partly built bridge that was going to go over the railway and marvelled at the number of people rushing about their business. They were like bees round a honey pot.

"Do you know of an American working round here?" He asked a man who looked as if he was unbolting rails from the road.

"Well, there's a thing; you're the second person what's asked that in the past two days. What's he done then, rob a bank?" The man guffawed.

Soper stroked his beard. "Do you know who was asking?"

"Can't say I've ever seen him afore, no. Not as filthy as some of 'em."

"Well, never mind, where can I find this person?"

"Who? The fellow asking for the American, or the American?" The man grinned.

"Don't be clever with me, my man," Soper admonished.

"He's down there, where the Priory ruins was."

"Thank you."

The constable made his way to a scene of great activity. Piles of bricks, scaffolding, wooden beams and sacks of sand and cement were everywhere. In the distance, he saw what he thought were brick makers. Men were scurrying around as if their lives depended on it.

"Are you an American?" enquired Soper, tapping a man on the shoulder.

Yank gave a big sigh. "Why are you asking?" He dusted off his hands.

"I've been told that you may have some knowledge of a Tobias Laird?"

"Tobias? I don't know anyone called Tobias, or Laird, come to that." Yank frowned, wondering whether to expand on this, but he decided the constable needed to earn his money.

"Do you know, or have you heard about a boy who has run away from home?"

How much should he divulge? How could he avoid getting himself and Mrs Grimley into trouble?

"There was a boy I heard about some time ago now," he admitted, "I didn't find out his name. I guess he could be who you're looking for."

"The lad I'm enquiring about is fourteen, and he lives to the north of the town. Have you visited any houses in that area? We've had reports of an American asking questions about him."

"No." He paused. "Are you sure he was an American?" How he wished he'd disguised his voice.

"Mr Laird's cook thought he was from there."

"I see. There might be another American round this way, although it's unlikely because I'm sure I'd have been told," Yank said. "But I haven't visited the north of the town," he lied. "I came here from Leigh, through Hildenborough."

"What happened to this young man you knew about?"

"I don't know. I guess he—"

"Yes?" Soper asked eagerly.

Yank was going to say he'd heard he had an interest in the new railway, but he thought this might give a clue about where he was now. "I was going to say he might have wanted to try his luck in London. You know what young people are like, they think the big city will solve all their problems."

"Um. Well, thank you, Mr—"

"I'm called Yank, or Big Yank. I don't think I've been of much help. What do you think is the reason for this young man wanting to leave home?" Yank thought he might find out if Thomas's ghastly father had confessed to the constable.

"I don't know, it's a mystery." Soper turned to leave. "But what you've told me just now is helpful."

Phew, that was close. Yank picked up his trowel and a brick and began slapping on the cement, heartily wishing he was from some other area – 'oop north' would have been a good place.

The fruit was all picked now, and the men were being given their money. Charlie glared at Thomas as they queued for their final payment.

"Why are you staring at me like that?" Thomas asked, glaring back.

"No reason."

Good, thought Thomas. Charlie couldn't challenge him without giving himself away. "Where are you going next?" he asked. *So I can avoid meeting you,* he thought to himself.

"Don't know, lad. What about you?"

"I'm thinking of some work to do with the railway."

Charlie laughed. "What, a little runt like you? You wouldn't stand a chance."

Thomas shrugged. "Got to get some money somehow. I had my money stolen, if you remember."

Charlie ignored him and moved up towards the farm door to get his pay.

Thomas was the last one to reach the door, and he found Mrs Acott standing behind her husband. "How are you going to manage from now on?" she asked him quietly.

"I'll find something, but I wonder if you could tell me where I could buy some clothes?"

"Look, you wait here, and I'll see what I can find. I have some food for you, too."

Thomas stared after her as she disappeared into the kitchen. How kind she was; there were some good people in the world, people just like Yank and Mrs Grimley.

Chapter Eleven

THOMAS SLEPT one more night in the hut after informing the farmer he was going to leave the next morning. When he enquired what he owed, the farmer very kindly said three pence, which Thomas thought was reasonable. That evening, he ate most of the food that Mrs Acott had packed for him – a lovely meat pie, some bread and a hardboiled egg. There was also an earthenware bottle filled with beer. Thomas had never tasted beer, but he drank it all the same and rather liked it.

He walked up the tracks, passing the almost completed Penshurst Station. Overall, he could walk right beside the workings instead of following the road; he just had to make sure he didn't get in the way. Progress was being made at pace, but he couldn't see how it would be finished next year – more likely in '42.

He often stopped to watch the navvies, marvelling at their strength and fortitude in the face of the hardships they encountered every day. Picks and shovels, cuttings and embankments, the spoils from one going to make the other. He knew for certain he could never do physical labour like that, but he was still determined to find some work linked to the railway.

He came to Jessop's Farm and asked if they had any jobs going, but his effort proved fruitless. One thing he could do now was walk without feeling tired, especially if he had food inside him. Mrs Acott had given him some old trousers that belonged to her husband. As he was a small man they fitted Thomas quite well, albeit a little bit big round the waist. She'd also given him a belt, a neatly patched shirt and some well-darned socks. He had his own coat, which, though well made, had now become so muddied and split in places that it could be taken for one purchased second hand. The same could be said of his shoes. What would his father say if he could see him now? He was unrecognisable, which was just what he wanted.

At Bough Beech, he watched the men working on the rails going over the newly constructed bridge. Then, only a few yards up the hill, the railway went under the road. Who, Thomas wondered, decided the route? Who said whether a road should go over or under the railway? It was governed by the rise of the land, he understood, but why a bridge and not an embankment? It was more or less following a straight line; nothing was skirted to avoid constructing a bridge. There was plenty of manpower, but someone had to design it. He was overwhelmed by the feats of engineering involved, and his admiration knew no bounds. The workings were much further advanced in this area.

He was by an inn called The Chequers and boldly went in and asked for some ale. He had never been in such a place before. With the two bridges less than half a mile apart, there were a great many men working in the area. He had to push his way to the serving table. He listened to the conversations going on around him, much of which he couldn't understand. Some of the men had strong accents and others spoke so badly he could only get the gist of what they were saying. He thought he heard them talking about a navvy being buried by falling earth or rocks. Yank had been right: he couldn't work with this type of person, but he was convinced there must be other jobs he could do.

On leaving the inn, he crossed the track by the partly built bridge and headed west. After half a mile, he came across a smithy. The forge was open, and he stood watching the blacksmith shoeing a horse.

"Hello, young man. Where are you off to?"

"Oh, I'm visiting an... an aunt in Edenbridge."

After his sojourn in the big wide world, Thomas could now lie quite glibly.

"Still got a fair way to go, then."

"You don't need any help, do you, sir?"

"Why, no, sorry. My two sons are apprenticed to me, and though we have quite a bit of work, what with the railway coming and them asking for odd items, we can cope with it all. Know anything about this type of work?"

"No, but I'm interested."

"You could try Clout's Farm." He pointed to his right. "Up there a few yards. He might have something, though I have me doubts. It's not the time of year for casual work."

Thomas had already discovered that, but he still hoped to find something he could do that was attached to the railway.

The blacksmith was proved right; there was no work at Clout's Farm. Thomas walked back to the bridge at Bough Beech and stood watching the bricklayers. Perhaps Yank had worked here at one time; he seemed to have worked everywhere. He wandered along the road that ran parallel to the railway and looked for somewhere to bed down for the night. Sleeping rough wasn't as daunting as it had once been, but it was getting colder. He ate the bread and cheese he had bought at the inn and thought of Yank and him saying, 'You can do anything if you have to.'

Thomas realised how kind Yank had been when he'd no need to take care of him. He wasn't justified in thinking he had been deserted. Yank wasn't responsible for him, and he and Mrs Grimley could be in trouble. He hoped his father would never find out what Yank had done.

Then his thoughts turned, as they frequently did, to his family. He shed a few tears before falling asleep in the cosy nest he had made for himself in a dip between two hedges. It was mercifully dry and far enough away from the navvies not to be disturbed.

The next day, he continued towards Edenbridge. The road turned away from the railway and he considered following it as it was easier walking, but he decided to stick with the track as there was not so much activity going on. He passed a brick and tile works and enquired if they had any work. Despondently, he walked on when the owner shook his head, informing him that farm work was all he was likely to get, and there wasn't much of that around this time of year.

As he walked, Thomas marvelled yet again at the obstacles that the engineers had to overcome. There might be plenty of manpower, but someone had to design it. He passed a small boy sitting close to the fencing. At first, he imagined he belonged to one of the navvy men, but looking around, he realised there was no one working nearby.

He retraced his steps and knelt in front of the lad. "Are you all right?"

The boy shook his head, and his long, matted hair swung to cover his face. He was wearing a thin shirt and ill-fitting trousers. No coat, no shoes.

"What's the matter with you?"

"I wanna eat." His eyes looked at Thomas hopefully.

Thomas felt in his pocket. He still had a bit of food left. "Here," he said, "you can have this."

The boy grabbed the bread and stuffed it into his mouth. Thomas looked at him pityingly. He was emaciated, just skin and bone, and his red-rimmed eyes were large in his hollow-cheeked face. The rags he wore barely covered him.

"What's your name?"

"Ayu."

"That's an unusual name. Do you live near here?"

"I dunno. Don' live nowhere."

"Have you any parents?"

The boy looked blank.

"Have you a father and mother, someone who looks after you?"

"There was a man and woman I was with, but they left me."

"Left you. What, just left you? Here?"

"Yeah."

'When?"

"Dunno."

Thomas tried to make sense of it. "Was it last night, before it got dark?"

"Yeah, think so. They leave me of an evening, but they come back."

"But not last night?"

"No."

"Does your… this man work on the railway?"

"Yeah, think so. They move round. I don't live nowhere. I ain't got no 'ouse to live in. I'd like a 'ouse."

Ayu stood up. His legs were so spindly that Thomas feared they wouldn't support him. He held out his hand and the boy grasped it. "Got something to drink?" he asked.

"No, 'fraid not, but if you come with me, I can buy you something at the next village."

The boy's large, sunken brown eyes lit up.

"But supposing your man and woman come to get you?"

"Don' think they want me – they say I stop 'em doing things and they'll leave me outside the work'ouse. I dunno what a work'ouse is, but an 'ouse is good, innit?"

"That's terrible, er, Ayu, and I don't think a workhouse is a good place at all." The wind was bitterly cold, and the boy was turning blue.

"Here," Thomas said, "you can have my coat."

He held it out and the boy slipped his skinny arms into the sleeves. The coat enveloped him, touching the ground and covering his ragged shirt and equally tattered trousers. How could anyone leave a boy in such a dreadful state?

"Come, let's see what we can find in the next village," Thomas said gently.

Chapter Twelve

THE PARISH CONSTABLE stood before Mr Laird in his study. "I have no news of any consequence for you, sir," he said. "I found the American, who's a bricklayer for the railway, but all he could say was that he met a boy of around sixteen who had been severely beaten, but he doesn't know where he is now, and he knew no one called Tobias."

"And did he come here to this house?"

"He says not. He came from Leigh through Hildenborough and is working in the south of the town."

Mr Laird stroked his whiskers. "I don't think the boy he met could be Tobias. Had you thought of going to Leigh to follow up this… this lead?"

"My assistant and I decided there was no point, as he didn't fit the description of Tobias that you gave me. Neither did we think your son would have been bearing the marks of someone who'd been badly beaten."

"Quite so, quite so." Mr Laird paused and frowned. "But could he have been attacked by someone else?"

"Someone else?" Soper thought this a strange remark. "Who?"

"Well, he might have been set upon by the navvies. I know they are… are, er, rough."

Soper didn't reply.

"Well, thank you, and please thank your assistant, too. I shall have to think about the situation again. It is very mysterious, don't you think?"

"Very mysterious," echoed Soper. He was sure Mr Laird knew more than he was letting on.

Yank stood up straight and stretched his back. He rubbed his rough hands down his dust-covered trousers and from his pocket took out a small meat pie and some cheese. Ten minutes was all they were allowed during the morning, and not even that if there was a time limit on the work to be done. He was just about to return to his task when he felt a tap on his shoulder.

"Someone looking for you, Yank."

Not another busybody enquiring about Thomas, surely. Would he ever be shot of the boy?

A portly, bewhiskered, well-dressed man, whose appearance was starkly out of place, was waiting just off the road in front of the partly constructed station, a horse tethered nearby.

"I'm known as Big Yank. You wish to speak to me for some reason?" He looked at the man enquiringly and held out his hand, which was ignored.

"You are an American, I believe."

"Sure am."

"A constable has told me that you met a boy in Leigh some time ago."

Yank's suspicion that this was Thomas's father was now confirmed, and he would have to be careful what he said. "Yes, briefly. His name was Thomas and he appeared to have been beaten." Yank wanted to say viciously beaten, cruelly beaten, anything to make this odious man acknowledge his crime.

"Attacked by navvies, no doubt?"

"I think not. They would likely have punched him, and he would be badly bruised and cut. His money would be stolen – his clothes as well in all probability. No, whoever did it was cruel and calculating, with an uncontrollable temper. This boy's back was a mass of wheals and—"

"Quite so. I just wanted to confirm what the constable told me. I cannot imagine what has happened to Tobias."

Yank looked at him, his head to one side. "And Tobias is?"

"My son."

"Has he run away?" He eyed the man up and down. "Why would he do that? I sure think your son must come from a good home."

"He certainly does." Laird was unaware what he had been trapped into confessing. He puffed out his chest so the fob on his gold watch chain swung from side to side and endeavoured to look at Yank with disdain. Yank held his gaze, putting into it all he had thought, and still did think about him.

They both knew that Thomas and Tobias were one and the same boy. Mr Laird eventually lowered his eyes. "I'll bid you good day."

He quickly strode off, mounted his horse and turned to make his way home. Yank stared after him, contempt written on his face, as the man crossed the track under the completed bridge.

Thomas and Ayu came to a hamlet called Lockhurst, where Thomas bought some food and drink, glad that he had enough money. But this wouldn't last long. Ayu clung to Thomas like a shadow. What was he to do with the boy? He had no idea of his age, and neither did the boy. He could be as young as five, but was probably around seven, with malnutrition stunting his growth.

"Look, Ayu, I can't look after you forever. I must find work to earn money."

"You woan leave me, will you?"

"But I don't know what to do with you." Then he thought of Yank. He hadn't left him when he was in distress.

"What about your parents... I mean your man or woman? How did they feed you?"

"They gave me bread sometimes."

"Only bread? Were you fed every day?"

"Yes." He paused. "I think."

"Anything else?"

"Some fruit if we were in the apple field." He frowned. "I don't know where they got it, but I used to drink the ale they brought."

Thomas sighed. It was obvious this boy was the son of a couple who lived from hand to mouth and had neither the money nor any idea of how to bring up a child. It was surprising that he had survived for so long.

"Why did they call you such a funny name? Were you named after your... your man?"

"No, his name's 'enry, and she's Kate. They used to shout at each other a lot – and at me."

They were squatting beside a place where the railway crossed a farmer's track. There was no bridge over or under it. Thomas supposed it was not worth the expense. The land was quite flat here so there was no need for a bridge or cutting. What would happen if the farmer's cattle strayed onto the line? Perhaps no one had thought of that, and the farmer had to put up with it. Thomas supposed the landowner lost any concern once he had his money from the railway company. Still, it could be fenced: he had seen plenty of carts and wagons with fencing posts and wire.

They had been sleeping rough for a week, which didn't seem to bother Ayu much, but Thomas was none too keen – not because he didn't want to (he had no choice), but he missed his coat. He would have to get some more clothes from somewhere. It even crossed his mind to steal them. Were these the depths he was sinking to?

He estimated that many parts of the railway from the Brighton line must be nearly complete by now. He heard some men talking about a long tunnel. He would love to go inside it and see how it was being built.

"Maybe the church can help us," Thomas said to Ayu. He thought of his one back in Tunbridge. His father gave money to it, but Thomas didn't know where that went. He was sure his father wouldn't condone assistance going to the destitute; more likely he would want it spent on a monument to glorify the church – even better if his name were mentioned.

They walked away from the track and stopped at the first church they came to. Thomas enquired at the vicarage if anyone could help them, but the housekeeper told him they did not deal with tramps, and to go away and get work, then they wouldn't have to beg. Thomas asked if she had any work he could do, but the door was slammed in his face.

That night, huddled together in a ditch, mercifully dry, Ayu started to cough and shiver. Thomas was sure he needed medicine, but he had hardly any money for food, let alone to pay for a doctor.

"I hurt 'ere," croaked Ayu, pointing to his throat and chest.

"I know, but I don't know what I can do. Can you walk with me when it gets light, and I'll see if I can find a pharmacist to help you?"

They curled up together to keep warm through the night, but in the morning, Ayu was no better. He could hardly breathe, his cough rattled in his throat and he was gasping for air.

"Look, I'm going to get some help."

"Don't go."

"I'll come back, I promise."

Leaving Ayu in tears, Thomas hurried to the next place, a hamlet called Mowhurst, and asked at a beer house if there was a pharmacy nearby. The landlord shook his head but said he might get some help from the house across the road, the one with the green door. This turned out to be the home of a midwife. Thomas explained the situation and the woman, who introduced herself as Mistress Keely, said she would assist them. She reached for a bottle on a shelf, added it to a black bag, put on a large cape and her bonnet and they left. On the way, Thomas explained how he came to know the sick boy.

"It's such a funny name," he said.

Mistress Keely smiled. "That's not his name. The boy's parents would just shout at him."

"What do you mean shout at him?"

"Hey, you." She saw the look on his face and smiled. "It's not unusual. He could have also been called Cumere, or something similar."

Thomas shook his head in disbelief.

By now they had reached the ditch where a distressed Ayu was lying. Mistress Keely knelt, lifted the boy into a sitting position and gave him something from her bottle. Thomas was a little alarmed about the contents, but he was in no position to protest. She gently laid the boy down and he continued wheezing between excruciating bouts of coughing, his thin body struggling to cope.

"What's wrong with him?" Thomas asked.

"I suspect it's pneumonia, and judging by the look of him, he won't recover because he's too malnourished."

With tears welling in his eyes, Thomas lay down beside Ayu, put his arms around him and held him close. "There, there," he murmured, "this kind lady has given you some medicine and you'll soon be all right. I will look after you; just go to sleep."

They sat like that for half an hour, and the midwife stayed with them. Eventually, Ayu's head fell to one side and the painful, laboured breathing stopped. The abrupt silence was overwhelming. Thomas removed his arm and gently laid the boy down. His body was so light he might have been lowering a newspaper. Mistress Keely held out her arms and Thomas went to her and howled. He couldn't stop. He wasn't just crying for Ayu, but for himself, his mother, his siblings and Yank, his only true friend.

At last, Mistress Keely said they must go to Edenbridge, as it was the nearest place they were likely to find a person in authority. "He will arrange for the boy to be buried," she explained.

The thought of having to pay for Ayu's funeral made Thomas feel sick. "But I have no money, only a few pence." He felt in his pocket to show her.

She grabbed his arm and shook her head. "He will be buried in a pauper's grave," she explained. "I expect you will have to give a constable all the details." Seeing Thomas's worried frown, she added, "I will help you. It's only a couple of miles to Edenbridge but we will call at my house first. Can you manage him?"

Thomas nodded. When they reached the cottage, Mistress Keely gave Thomas something to eat and drink and then they walked into the town, with Thomas still carrying the boy. Just as the midwife had promised, once they'd informed the authorities, poor Ayu was no longer their responsibility.

* * *

Later that evening, Mistress Keely and Thomas sat together in front of the fire in her cottage. After leaving Edenbridge, Thomas was still clearly distressed, so the midwife allowed him to remain deep in his thoughts, while offering him the comfort of her company. It was obvious that until now, death had played little part in his life.

"Perhaps you can tell me a little bit about yourself," she said with a gentle smile. "I must say, you are a bit of a mystery to me."

As usual, Thomas wondered how much he should reveal. The desire to unburden himself was strong. He needed someone to confide in, like he had with Yank, but could he trust this woman? She had kindly accompanied him to the police station, overseeing all that had to be done, so that he only had to inform the constable how he had met Ayu and how long he had known him for. The constable had displayed no surprise that a sick young boy was wandering around on his own with no one to look after him. "It happens all the time," he'd stated matter-of-factly. Thomas was appalled.

"Well?" Mistress Keely pressed.

"I don't know what to say." He frowned and thought of a way to change the subject. "Why are you called Mistress and not Mrs?"

"I'm not married, and Mistress is a courtesy title

because I am a midwife. You can call me Jane if you like."

"Oh, no, I couldn't possibly do that. That wouldn't be right."

"What would you like to call me, then?"

Thomas considered that Mistress Keely seemed such a long name, but then so was Mrs Grimley's. "All right, I'll call you Jane," he said, "but I would rather call you Miss Jane, if you don't mind."

"Very well," she said. "Now, will you tell me about yourself? I can tell you've had a good schooling, but your clothes have seen better days. Where do you come from?"

"I don't want to tell you that because I have run away from home," Thomas replied. "I wanted to do work connected with the railway, but I'm not strong enough." He told Miss Jane about trying to lift the barrow and she laughed. "There doesn't seem to be anything else I can do," he added, lifting his shoulders and then letting them drop disconsolately.

"So, did you run away because your father wouldn't let you work on the railway? Did your parents want you to do something else when you left school?"

"My father has never said what he wants me to do."

Jane studied Thomas's face and deduced theirs was not a happy relationship.

"I ran away on the spur of the moment, and I

didn't think about how hard it would be to get work. In fact, I didn't think at all. I just needed… wanted to get away. I met a bricklayer who worked for the railway, and he looked after me for a while at his landlady's, and then… and then he had to leave to work in Tunbridge."

Tears filled Thomas's eyes. Jane put out her hands and rested them on his. "And then I saw Daw… someone, and I knew my father had sent him to look for me, so I left."

"What are you going to do now?"

"I need money. I'm determined to work on the railway at some point, but there's not much casual work on the land at the moment, and that seems to be done by the men who work for the farmers full time." He glanced up at the midwife. "You don't know of anything round here I could do, do you?"

"No, certainly not around here, but there might be something in Edenbridge."

Thomas gazed into the fire and watched the flames curl around the wood and coal. A kettle hung from a hook, and a saucepan rested on a trivet on the hearth. Jane said he could stay with her for two nights, and he offered her the few coppers he had, which she refused because she said he would need them. He tried to insist that he couldn't impose on her without paying, and they both chuckled when she replied that he could hardly help her with delivering babies.

When the laughter died down, Thomas decided to

seize the opportunity to ask Miss Jane how babies were born. He knew there was a great deal of rushing about, and that jugs of hot water seemed to be central to the situation, but no matter who he asked back at home, nobody would tell him or Lizzie exactly what happened and how babies came to grow in their mother's stomach.

Jane explained all she could and grinned when she saw his face redden. Thomas sat for some time remembering how his present situation had come about in the first place. "Can you now tell me what fornication means?" he asked.

The following day, they went to Edenbridge. Jane knew the pharmacist and asked if he had any work for a young, educated boy, but there wasn't anything for him. The midwife noticed him looking Thomas up and down – he obviously didn't like what he saw.

"Let's see if we can find you some better clothes, Thomas," she said once they had left the shop, "that might help your case."

She held up her hand as soon as he brought up money. "I will see to it. They won't be new, but they will be better than some of the clothes you have at the moment."

Luckily there was a market on, and they studied all the tables. "Have you decent underclothes?" she asked. He nodded but said they were not very clean, and that he had two shirts in the same condition.

"You need some better trousers and shoes."

After rummaging around various tables, they took home their purchases and Jane laid them out on the table. "Now," she said, "I have to go and visit two ladies. You take off all your clothes and wash yourself. There's a tin bath on the wall outside and you can put it in front of the fire and fill it. I will be out for well over an hour, maybe two, so you will have plenty of time to make yourself presentable. Try on the clothes we have bought, and if some want repairing, I will see to them later, and I'll also wash the rest."

As she went to shut the front door after her, she called, "and remember to put the cold water in the bath first."

* * *

Septimus Laird was in his study, elbows on his desk, his head in his hands. For the first time in his life, he felt helpless. His wife no longer showed him the deference he expected, and Elizabeth barely spoke to him. He could see from her eyes that she'd lost her respect for him. The servants seemed to regard him in a hostile manner, too, though he couldn't pinpoint a particular incident that supported this. Only Cook seemed to treat him as she always had.

From his talk with the American, it seemed

obvious that Tobias was trying to get work, probably on the railway. He knew his son was fascinated by it, although they had never talked about it. Septimus couldn't remember discussing anything with his eldest son, or any of his other children for that matter, unless it was to do with their lessons.

What should he do now? Get Dawkins to search for him along the track to – where was it? – Red Hill village. Or could he have gone the other way towards Ashford? He had read that the railway was being built in different stretches, each with its own contractor, so finding Tobias would be hard. If it wasn't, what would he do when his son was found? Everyone would learn why he had left in the first place. Perhaps it would be best to leave things as they were while making out he had done all he could to find him. Amelia needn't know he had discovered some information about the American. Perhaps the hard life that Tobias had to live now would drive him back home. But would that satisfy his wife? She was so scathing in her comments. Damn the woman, she should know her place.

When Jane returned to the cottage, Thomas stood before her.

"Now, you do look presentable," she said, studying him carefully and asking him to turn around.

"It's good to be clean and feel... feel." He searched for a word. He was going to say civilised. "Apart from splashing my face and hands with water from streams and ponds, I haven't had a good wash since I left Leigh. I washed my hair, too. Do you think I have a better chance of finding work now?"

"I'm sure you have. What *would* you like to do, apart from working on the railway?"

"I really have no idea. As I told you, I'm not as robust as I thought. I even found apple picking exhausting. Now I look more presentable, perhaps I could work in a shop."

The only trouble with that, Thomas thought, *is that I might be recognised by someone.* Earning money was the priority, so he pushed that thought away.

"Yes, I think you will stand a better chance now. Stay here for another night and then you can walk into Edenbridge again." Miss Jane gave a sigh. "I shall miss you, Thomas," she added.

Choking back the tears, which were coming readily to his eyes, Thomas gulped and replied, "Me too."

Part Two

Chapter Thirteen

TAKING his leave of Miss Jane, and tearfully thanking her for her kindness, Thomas strode briskly into Edenbridge. His step was light, and he was confident he could find somewhere on the high street that needed an assistant who could read and write.

The road he took went under the railway before turning right into the town. He had tried a smithy on the outskirts, but he'd had no more luck there than he had at Bough Beech. He also came across a shop that sold old clothes, but he didn't like the look or the smell of the shopkeeper. The pharmacist, he knew, had nothing, even though he now looked more presentable. Across the road he saw a sign advertising the Plough Inn, and he even enquired in there if they needed any help, but this only brought forth yet more disappointment.

Dispirited, he got himself something to eat and

drink. This left him with only six pennies to his name and brought home the urgency of finding employment. He sat on a milestone just past the station, which was mainly a wooden construction.

Most of the activity seemed to be about a quarter of a mile up the line where there was a cutting. He finished his pie and drank his ale, which he had come to enjoy. Out of curiosity, he followed the track and watched as the cutting began to take shape. He tried to look as inconspicuous as possible.

It was while he was watching that he heard a terrific explosion that scared him and made him seek shelter. He had heard these explosions plenty of times in recent weeks, but they were not quite as close or as loud as this one. He saw a commotion ahead and a group of navvies rushing towards the far end of the cutting. Thomas ran along behind them. A man was lying on the ground beside a wagon full of debris. He crept closer to see what had happened.

Apparently, after the blasting, a rock had fallen on him, and he was now lying on the ground and screaming in pain. Without any care, the navvies hauled him to one side and laid him beside the track, where the man writhed in agony, clutching his right arm. Thomas felt sick and asked a navvy standing beside him if they were going to get a doctor. He was told it was unlikely one would come.

"I'll go and try, if you like."

"Yeah, but don't be s'prised if you don't get nowhere."

Thomas hurried away, the screams from the man ringing in his ears. He went back into The Plough and asked where the nearest doctor lived. With no time to spare, he ran to his destination on the outskirts of town.

After much persuasion and his six pence, Thomas managed to get the doctor to attend the accident on his horse. Meanwhile, Thomas had to walk back. When he arrived at the scene, he discovered that the man had a broken arm. He'd also fractured three ribs. The doctor bound him up and left.

"Did well there, lad. The doctor didn't seem too keen to be here, but he didn't ask for no money."

Thomas was going to admit that he had paid him, but he thought it best to keep that quiet lest he draw too much attention to himself. While he was standing amongst the navvies, some patting his shoulder, painfully at times, and generally making a bit of a fuss of him, he saw a well-dressed man approach.

"Who's that?" he asked.

"He's a sub-contractor on this section of the line," said an elderly man almost bent double in stature. "His name's Hubber. We heard he took the place of Mr Parr what went bankrupt."

Mr Hubber was questioning the men about the accident. He wanted to know what had caused it, whose fault it was and, when it was explained it was a falling rock, why everyone had not cleared the area. "You know there's always the chance of falling rocks or trees," he said. "What saved him from being more badly hurt?"

One of the men explained that a nearby wagon had partly shielded the navvy. As he listened, Thomas felt he was part of the scene and quite forgot he had nothing to do with it.

"Who's this?" Mr Hubber enquired, seeing a young lad who did not seem to fit the usual navvy type.

"Oh, that's the lad what said he'd get a doctor. Very quick he was, too."

"What's your name?"

"Thomas."

Mr Hubber nodded his head and turned to go, but Thomas ran up to him, seizing his chance. "Sir, you don't have any work I can do, do you? I know I can't do what the men and boys do, but if there's anything else, I'm very willing."

Mr Hubber thought for a moment. "Come and see me in the morning and I'll see what I can do."

"Oh, thank you, sir!" he called as the man mounted his horse and rode away.

When he had gone, Thomas asked a boy where he would find Mr Hubber next morning.

"Nowt t'noo. 'e rides oop 'n doon t'line alt t'ime, you joost 'ave t' look for 'im."

Thomas just about gathered what he had said – Mr Hubber was hard to find!

That night, he found an empty barn to sleep in, and he could only hope the owner wouldn't come and turf him out. Next morning, he walked back into the town, but this time along the track, searching for the type of building a man as important as Mr Hubber might have as an office. He passed the station, close to where the accident had taken place, and came across a wooden hut near a large, incomplete building that looked as if it might be a hotel one day. He stopped to question a navvy, who Thomas thought was Irish and, therefore, would be easier to understand. He confirmed that the wooden hut was indeed Mr Hubber's office. As he went over to it, he noticed the man's horse tethered to one side, almost out of sight.

"Come in." Mr Hubber looked up with a frown as Thomas knocked on the open door. "Yes?"

"Good morning, sir. You said you might be able to find me work."

Mr Hubber's frown deepened. "Oh, was this when you attended the accident yesterday?"

"Yes," Thomas replied.

"Ah, yes. Well, sit down." He pointed to a stool beside his table. "What's your name again?"

"My name's Thomas... Thomas Layton," he replied, hurriedly thinking of a surname. "I've come from London. My parents have both died, so I must look for work. I'm fascinated by the railway so I thought I would come south and see if there was anything. Unfortunately, I'm not strong enough for the physical work the navvy boys do." Thomas could now spin a yarn to fit any situation – he just had to utilise his memory and watch his voice.

"That's true."

Mr Hubber grinned as he looked Thomas up and down. Most of the workers he dealt with could hardly string a sentence together or had accents he was only just getting used to. This lad seemed out of the ordinary. He handed him a piece of paper. "Read it," he instructed.

"To Mr Hubber, from Charles Fortune. Date—"

"Never mind all that. Read the content."

"On the twentieth instant, several wagons loaded with explosives will be coming to you from Tunbridge. I will arrange for the wagon to be accompanied by a man to make sure that it is carried with safety. I hope that—"

"That's fine." He handed Thomas a sheet of paper and a pencil. "Take down what I say."

Thomas slowly wrote down what Mr Hubber said next, which was a response to Charles Fortune's note.

After scrutinising his work, he said to Thomas, "You have a very clear hand and good spelling. I'll take you on as a runner. It won't be hard physical work, but you will have to cover a great deal of ground on occasion and be quick. Do you think you can do that?"

"Oh, yes, sir. I'll love it, sir." Thomas was almost leaping up and down with excitement.

Mr Hubber gave a wry smile. "Let's hope you'll still be saying that when you arrive back exhausted from a job and I immediately send you off somewhere else."

"I shan't mind, and I'll do my best. Thank you, sir. I hope you don't mind my asking, but how much will I be paid? I shall have to find lodgings, you see."

The older man contemplated the question. "How about, er, three and sixpence a week, payable on Fridays?"

Thomas nodded, too excited to worry whether it was a decent wage or not.

"I would advise you, Layton, not to get involved with the young lads. Keep out of their way because they will involve you in fights and steal everything you own. Try to find a decent place to live. I will endeavour to keep you informed of my whereabouts so you can find me more easily."

Thomas looked about him, excited at what he had achieved. "What shall I do now, sir?" he asked. "Look for somewhere to stay? Is Edenbridge a good place, or shall I go nearer to Red Hill village?"

"No, practically all the work is done in that direction. I think round here will do for the present, but mind, occasionally you might have to stay in different places overnight, and I shan't always be here. I have other offices along the line. There is a very big project at Cooksey, with the building of the tunnel." He stood up. "I hope you find somewhere satisfactory."

Mr Hubber's warning to him about losing the clothes he was wearing reminded Thomas of Yank's similar words of advice. Wouldn't Yank be proud of him? He couldn't wait to see the tunnel being built. How thrilling that would be.

Feeling quite light-headed, he skipped towards the main street and enquired in a shop about places to stay. A young girl overheard him and told him to follow her, as her mum took in lodgers. She said her name was Anna and asked him what his was, his age and where he came from. By the time they reached her house, Thomas had divulged all he thought she needed to know.

"Mother, this is Thomas Layton and he's looking for somewhere to stay," she said. "He's a runner for the railway and he's starting tomorrow."

"You're lucky. I have a room available as one of my lodgers has gone to find work in Tunbridge. Do you want food?"

"Mr Hubber said I might not be in this area all the time, so I can't say if I'll need to eat regularly. Is that all right?" Thomas was afraid she wouldn't agree to have him. The house was so much nicer than Mrs Grimley's cottage, and he had also taken a shine to

Anna. She was very pretty, with long brown hair beneath her white cap, and vivid blue eyes that twinkled when she laughed.

"I think I can manage that, but you'll have to give me warning. I don't want to prepare a meal that will then go to waste."

"I'll do my best, Mrs… I'm sorry, Anna didn't tell me your name."

"Mrs Fishlock."

"I'll show Thomas his room, shall I, Mother?" Anna held out her hand, which Thomas was delighted to hold.

So began one of the happiest periods of Thomas's life. He enjoyed his work, though he found it tiring at times, and thoughts of his previous life came into his mind less and less.

At Christmas, Mrs Fishlock cooked a goose and Thomas revealed his birthday was on New Year's Eve and that he would be fifteen. He hadn't previously mentioned his age to Anna, and he'd been tempted to add a year, though he changed his mind. She already thought of him as mature.

He loved staying at Mrs Fishlock's, and he was beginning to fall in love with Anna, although he had not yet realised it. When he had free time, mostly on a Sunday, he and Anna would go for walks. She told him about the dame's school that she had attended and how, when she had learned to read, she realised that her teacher, Mistress Dolby, didn't know much about anything other than reading. She persuaded her mother to find her somewhere else and she was now at a small school, where, apart from her and one other student, all the pupils were boys.

"Trouble is, no one thinks girls are worth educating, but I'm better than most of them," she boasted, to which Thomas replied he could well imagine that.

"You don't believe that about girls, do you?"

"No, my…" He was about to say his sister Lizzie was very clever. Anna didn't notice his slip. One thing he could say in his father's favour was that all his children were well tutored.

Anna told Thomas how her father had died when she was ten, along with her baby brother. "Mother had two miscarriages, so I am an only child, like you."

Thomas wasn't sure what a miscarriage was, but he deduced from what Miss Jane had told him that it must be something to do with losing a baby before it was born.

* * *

It was a Sunday in late March, and Thomas and Anna were heading off for a walk beside the River Eden. It was extremely cold, and Anna was wrapped up warmly. Thomas had bought himself some more presentable clothes and another pair of second-hand boots, which he had tried to keep for his Sunday best. However, his other pair was so worn after the amount of walking he had to do on rough tracks that he now had to wear his new ones all the time.

Mrs Fishlock watched from her window as the two youngsters began their walk. The wind caught Anna's hair from under her fur hat, which Thomas had bought her for her birthday. Anna's mother was a little troubled, as she could see they were becoming very fond of each other. She liked Thomas, as he was so polite and considerate, but Anna was a little wayward and she didn't want her getting into a situation she couldn't cope with. She decided she must have a serious talk with her. Anna was not as worldly wise as she thought she was, and Thomas, kindly as he appeared, might not be knowledgeable about young girls. There was something strange about him. What she observed did not quite fit with what he had told her.

Chapter Fourteen

IT SEEMED to Thomas that he had left home a lifetime ago. Mr Hubber was pleased with his work – at least, he hadn't said he wasn't. He avoided the navvies where possible, though he was tempted at times to see exactly what they were doing. Thomas still thought of his mother, and of Lizzie and his other siblings, but they had ceased to be at the forefront of his mind. He had settled down to a steady life and was no longer having to live on his wits.

On one of their Sunday walks, he and Anna went along Hilders Lane and past Hilders House, where they had to cross the railway. Thomas explained about the bridges, cuttings and embankments. Anna wasn't very interested; she thought the countryside would never recover from the desecration. Thomas tried to explain how it would make life so much easier for everyone. People could go to the seaside, up to

London to work and even travel to the Continent much more easily, but Anna wasn't convinced.

They crossed the Kent Brook and then turned north and had to cross yet another bridge, where, to Anna's disgust, Thomas waxed lyrical all over again.

"Thomas, you do go on so. It's a pity that you can't design a railway all by yourself and live beside it forever."

"If only I could, Anna, I would be in heaven."

"Oh, Thomas, surely not!"

They reached a path between two farms and entered Batchelorswood Bank.

"Mother and I often come up here for a walk. It's lovely, isn't it? Look, I've got two slices of pie and a drink that she gave us. Did you bring anything?"

"Only some fruit. It's what I bought yesterday and didn't finish."

When they had eaten, Anna said she was going to climb a tree. Thomas wasn't happy about this; one, because it was not seemly for a young lady to climb trees, and two, she might fall.

"I shall be all right. I have climbed trees before, you know."

This wasn't strictly true, as her mother felt the same as Thomas and had forbidden her to do so.

Anna tucked her dress into her drawers as best she could and looked around for a tree with a suitably low branch on which she could start her climb.

"I wish you wouldn't," Thomas said, alarmed.

She ignored him and airily waved from the first sturdy branch she managed to reach. After adjusting her skirts, she reached for a higher branch. Grasping one with her left hand, she reached out her right to grab the one nearest to it. This didn't prove as strong, and, as Anna held it, it snapped.

Thomas was standing below her and managed to break her fall, but she twisted her ankle as she hit the ground.

"You stupid, stupid girl," he shouted, as he picked her up and carelessly shook her. "Look what you've done. I told you not to do it. Now your mother will blame me for not looking after you."

Anna was crying, not so much from the pain, though her ankle did hurt, but because Thomas was speaking to her so harshly.

"I'm s… sorry," she sniffed. "Don't, don't b… be cross with me."

Thomas held her close, conscious of her heart beating rapidly against his chest. He stroked her hair and kissed it.

"Don't cry, Anna. I'm sorry I shouted at you, but you frightened me so."

Anna looked up at him with her big, tear-framed eyes, and poor Thomas was lost. He kissed her on the lips, gently at first and then more passionately. All the while, the strangest feeling came over him.

"Promise me you won't do anything like that again." He pushed her away gently, embarrassed.

Anna flung her arms around his waist. "I promise, but you do love me, don't you?"

"Yes, I think I do."

When they arrived home, both Thomas and a limping Anna were scolded and banned from going out together on their own. Thomas thought this might be difficult to enforce but he didn't want to upset his landlady, even though Anna winked at him as if to say she thought much the same.

* * *

Today, Thomas was to go to Cookseys Tunnel near Bletchingley. Yank had told him it was over a thousand yards long and needed many shafts for the steam from the engines to escape through. Thomas told Mrs Fishlock that he would be gone for some time and not to prepare meals for him – he would try to let her know when he would be back.

"You'll be gone for ages, won't you?" Anna said, after hearing the news. She wiped away the tears that were already running from her eyes.

"I really don't know. I have to follow Mr Hubber. I'll probably have to take lodgings nearer that way."

Anna was distraught. "You'll leave here forever – and never come back!" she wailed.

"That is very unlikely, isn't it, Anna? There's no need to be so melodramatic."

Anna thought she had every right to be melo… whatever the word was.

The night after her accident, Mrs Fishlock had spoken to her daughter about Thomas. Her ankle was badly bruised, but her mother bandaged it up and it was practically back to normal in a little over a week. During this time, Anna had been quite subdued, and though she was still in love with the lodger, she tried not to get too close to him in case the thing happened that her mother had warned her about. She still wasn't quite sure what she must or must not do, or what would happen.

"I shall be back. I might get some time off and return for a day," Thomas said, realising how much he would miss Anna, too. "I must go where the work is," he explained.

Yank came into his mind then, and how it had felt when he'd said he had to move on.

"I know how you feel, Anna, but I haven't moved away yet. Don't cry." He patted her arm. "I would like you to do something for me. I have saved some money and I would like you to look after it. Will you do that?"

"Yes," she sniffed.

"Tell you what – I'll bring you back a present."

"You won't forget me, will you?"

"How could I do that?" he said, and he kissed her on her cheek.

* * *

It was over five miles to Cookseys Farm, but the distance no longer held the dread that it once had. On his way to Godstone, Thomas noticed how many more workers were around. More and more trucks passed him going in both directions. Some of the larger wagons had huge tree trunks on them. He puzzled over what these were for. Brick making machines were everywhere, but he could understand why that was: a tunnel would need plenty of those. Thomas noticed the nearly built station and began to wonder where he might stay for the night. Judging by the number of men in the area, he thought it might be a ditch somewhere. After the comfortable accommodation he enjoyed at Mrs Fishlock's, he did not relish the thought. Besides, he had to look presentable now.

Mr Hubber told Thomas that he was moving to the tunnel workings and, knowing how interested his assistant was, he explained a bit about how the tunnel was being constructed. "The men have to blast and bore through rock and clay. It is more complicated than clearing for a cutting or making an embankment."

"Who designed it?"

"A Mr Simms."

"Have you met him?"

"Briefly, on more than one occasion. He has a

145

great deal of experience. This is not the first tunnel he's designed."

Thomas desperately wanted to meet this man – well, not meet him, but at least look at him. He must be a wonderful person.

"We have many experienced men building the tunnels; bricklayers, of course, excavators, miners—"

"Miners! So, that's what those big trunks are for – pit props. I did wonder. I suppose the miners come from Wales and Yorkshire and Nottingham."

Mr Hubber marvelled, as he had on many occasions, at the knowledge this boy possessed. Not only was he intelligent, but he must have been to a good school. He'd certainly been well taught by somebody, and he was an avid reader to boot. After his parents had died, why was there no one to take care of him?

"How do they—?"

"That's enough for now, Thomas. I must get on. It's going to be a very busy time. It was hoped the railroad to Tunbridge would be open by next March, but I doubt that. It's midsummer now and there's many loose ends to tie up in the various sections. They must all link up seamlessly."

* * *

When Thomas had almost reached the area where the tunnel workings were, his nose told him what sort of scene would greet him. There were the navvies in their makeshift huts and tents, and what seemed to be frenzied activity everywhere. Men were rushing in all directions; the wagons that had passed him with the tree trunks on them were being unloaded, while smaller carts and wagons had shovels, picks, trowels, wheelbarrows and other items needed for the many trades being employed. There was even a cart loaded with hay for the horses. Thomas couldn't see any horses, other than those bringing goods. He wondered where they were and what they were needed for.

He jumped as someone behind him shouted, "Get out the way, boy," and promptly rushed past him pushing a low, four-wheeled wagon.

Thomas's next task was to find Mr Hubber, then he would have to think about somewhere to stay. He looked around him, seeking some kind of office or his tethered horse. He was finding it hard to concentrate when all he wanted to do was stand and watch what was going on all around him. He asked a man, typically dirty, dishevelled and in a rush, where he might find his boss.

"Dunno, prob'ly oop top."

"Of course, why didn't I think of that?" Thomas muttered to himself.

He could see the tunnel entrance ahead, but he was in a deep cutting and had to find his way up to the top. He was going to ask someone, but each trade seemed intent on their contribution. Even the navvies, whose work, Thomas thought, was soul destroying, appeared wholly focused on their particular tasks.

Some of the workmen were differently dressed, and one or two men, more smartly attired, stood studying files. He wondered where they were lodging – not with the navvies, he was sure of that. He'd soon find out if he was going to be here for some time. He hugged himself – what joy!

Chapter Fifteen

"I'm here, Mr Hubber," Thomas said, as he tapped on the open door of the hut. "Isn't it wonderful here?"

Mr Hubber, who had just been told they were behind schedule and might have to work on Sundays, was not in the mood for 'wonder'. No doubt the local vicar would object and there'd be more trouble.

"Now, Thomas," he said brusquely. "I want you to familiarise yourself with this whole area, so when I send you somewhere, you will know where to go and what I am talking about. I don't want you wasting time looking for people or places."

Thomas was about to tell him he couldn't think of anything he'd rather do than wander around, but Mr Hubber quickly continued. "You must be very careful," he warned. "Don't go into the tunnel workings unless you have someone with you; that is, someone who understands what is being done down there. Some of the men and boys are very rough and careless, and there will be frequent blasting going on. I'll give you a Note of Authority to show. But first of all, as you are already at the summit, you may as well look at the shafts."

His Note of Authority carefully and proudly put away in an inside pocket, Thomas went along to the first shaft nearest the tunnel entrance at the Tunbridge end. Here he saw a large wooden structure with winding gear on top of it, with ropes leading to a wheel, which went down a large hole. Nearby, a neatly dressed man was talking to two scruffy lads about Thomas's age. He was pointing at the hole, and when he had finished speaking, he turned and spotted Thomas, who reached for his Authority.

"No need for that, young Layton. I've heard all about you from Hubber. Very impressed he was."

"Oh!" Thomas couldn't believe Mr Hubber had said that.

"I gather he wants me to explain what is going on up here." He indicated for Thomas to come closer. "The shafts are around nine to ten feet across," he said, sweeping his hand in front of him. "And they were bored by this machine called a gin, which, as you can see, is powered by horses and ropes attached to a wheel. Eventually, the shafts will allow the steam to escape from the locomotives, but as the tunnelling immediately beneath us has been completed, they now provide the men and boys with a means of getting down to the bottom of the tunnel and bringing up the displaced earth and rocks. They offload it, and it goes to make embankments in other places. We're nearing the end of the tunnel now, so all the embankments will probably have been finished round here, and the spoils will be sent elsewhere."

At that moment, a boy came up in a type of bucket. He climbed out, shovelled the debris he had been sitting on and filled a barrow held by another boy, who then pushed it away. The first boy then climbed back into the bucket and disappeared from view.

"Do they ever fall out?" Thomas asked, half joking.

"Yes, quite often. Navvies are very often killed or injured during the construction of tunnels." This was said with some indifference, as if it were to be expected and nothing could be done about it. It reminded Thomas of the way the constable had spoken about the death of young Ayu.

"Have you got any questions, young man?"

"Hundreds," Thomas said with a grin, "but I can't stay for too long, as Mr Hubber wants me to see as much as I can, so that I'll quickly know where to go."

"Have you found anywhere to stay?" Mr Hubber enquired when Thomas reported back.

"No, sir. I was going to look when you had finished with me here."

"Well, you'd better go now. It won't be easy as there are well over a thousand men on this site, and many of the more skilled ones don't want to live in the manner of the navvy."

"I'll see you tomorrow then, sir," Thomas replied.

Thomas tried Cookseys Farm, but, as Mr Hubber had warned, all the rooms she had were taken by the more discerning workers, probably sub-contractors. The next place he tried was South Park, but he was not successful there, either, and for the same reason. Thomas walked farther away from the track and came to a farm called Coldharbour. Here, he was appraised by an unfriendly lady farmer. He gathered that, like Mrs Grimley, she wasn't enamoured with the railway, or anything connected with it, and she refused to have anyone staying on her land. Her labourers were told to turf off anyone who tried to camp there.

With as much charm as he could muster, Thomas said that he would be no trouble, and that he was employed by Mr Hubber. She did not know who that was, but noticing how well Thomas spoke, she showed him a small attic room, which had just enough room for a wooden bed. "You can have this," she said begrudgingly.

The next few days saw Thomas travelling backwards and forwards, not to mention up and down, around the tunnel area. This meant he occasionally had to walk to the Red Hill end of the tunnel. Less often he travelled two miles in the other direction towards Tunbridge. What he desperately wanted to do was go *into* the tunnel and see exactly how it was being constructed. Just being told was not good enough for his enquiring mind. He did pick up bits of information on his journeys, but he wanted to see for himself. Occasionally, he met miners who would stop, albeit briefly, to tell him what they had been doing. They had different jobs, such as hacking away after a blasting, just as they would hack the coal. Others would be tasked with shoring up the roof of an excavation.

Because there were so many skilled workmen on the site, a sort of village had grown around the shafts. Thomas came across a butcher's, three grocers and more than one shop selling a variety of goods. He found this very handy when he needed food or a drink, although the navvies still had their revolting camps.

He decided to keep trying to persuade his boss to send him inside the tunnel on some professional pretext, but really just so he could investigate what happened down there.

Eventually, that day came. "Right, young Layton," Mr Hubber said to him. "I know you have been very patient, but tomorrow I need you to take these papers from Mr Cubitt to Charles Prentiss. Prentiss is one of the engineers, and he has worked on other tunnels for the railway. I have warned him you are fascinated with everything to do with railways, so he might – I say might – humour you, but you must not hinder him. Though the tunnel is almost finished, there is activity in and around it, and you could easily be injured by some unexpected occurrence, especially if you're not concentrating on what is being said." Mr Hubber wagged his finger at Thomas as he said this.

"I shall be very careful, sir, I promise."

"Do you know who Mr Cubitt is?"

"No, sir."

Mr Hubber wouldn't have been surprised if Layton had replied yes and given chapter and verse about the great man.

"He has previously worked on the line to Brighton for the London and Croydon Railway," he explained. "He is now the Chief Engineer for the South Eastern Railway to Dover."

Oh, that's what I want to be, Thomas mused. *One day, maybe.*

* * *

So far, Thomas had only been 'oop top', as he now thought of it, and he was able to find his way to his

154

lodgings without having to go down to the railway level.

That night, he barely slept from excitement over what he was about to learn. He knew quite a bit already from watching and asking questions of anyone who would stop long enough to talk to him, but now he would be witnessing everything first hand.

Next morning, he started singing as he made his way from his lodgings to the tunnel entrance. He searched for a man in smart clothing but could see no such person. A horn sounded and men and boys rushed past him.

"Don't just stand there, run!" a man shouted, before roughly grabbing Thomas's arm. There was a loud noise and a whoosh as the displaced air came surging out. It hit Thomas in the back, taking him from the man's grasp.

"Didn't you know what that horn meant?"

"I've heard it before, but I didn't know exactly what it signalled. I've only just arrived. I'm here to meet Mr Prentiss."

"Well, someone should've warned you." With that, the man walked off.

Meanwhile, clouds of dust swirled about him, and men and boys dashed back into the tunnel. When everything began to clear, he saw a man coming towards him, who he correctly assumed was Mr Prentiss.

"Are you Layton?"

"Yes, sir, but call me Thomas." He thought he was perhaps being a bit brazen, but Mr Prentiss made no comment. "I must give you this." He removed the papers from a folder and handed them to the engineer, who put them inside a file he was carrying.

"Did you hear the explosion?"

"Yes."

"Were you frightened?"

"Well, sir, not so much frightened as surprised. I didn't know what was going to happen."

"Didn't you hear the horn?"

"Yes, but I'd only just arrived, and I didn't know exactly what it was for. If everyone hadn't come rushing out, I would have—"

"I'm sorry, I should've been here. I didn't expect you so early."

Thomas didn't tell him he would have been even earlier had he not exercised some restraint.

"Why was there a need for an explosion? I would have thought that would all be over by now."

"Because they found a fault further inside, and they needed to repair it. I have to inspect it later, and I'm hoping it's only a small fault." He smiled wryly at Thomas. "Mr Hubber said you were keen to inspect the work that's going on in there." He turned towards the tunnel, and before Thomas could reply, added, "Right, follow me."

Once inside, they stood behind a man finishing off a line of bricks. Thomas immediately thought of Yank.

"As you can see, this bricklayer is the last man to finish here at the entrance. Behind him, the miners would have been putting up boards that overlapped from the top down to the track bottom."

"Like a lining."

"Exactly."

They moved on. "The miners deal with their own excavations and load the debris onto wagons," Mr Prentiss explained.

Thomas looked around him and caught sight of a small wagon by the tunnel wall opposite. "I saw these a few days ago," he observed, "and I wondered what they were for."

He tried to take everything in so he could lie in bed that night and dream about it. They had now reached what he thought must be the shaft. A boy was descending in a bucket.

"I should think he must be one of the last boys to do that," Thomas commented.

"Yes, you're probably right. I think I'll leave you now. Have you found it of interest?"

"Oh, yes, thank you. It's so fascinating. I would like to know more. I want to be a railway engineer one day."

"Good for you. You'll have plenty of work when you've qualified. Many new lines are being built in this part of the country alone. There's the one to

Tunbridge Wells from Tunbridge, and, I suspect, when parliament finally agrees to it, a new terminus in London that will bring another line down to the coast through the town."

While Mr Prentiss strode deeper into the tunnel, Thomas left to report back to Mr Hubber.

Chapter Sixteen

For the next few months, Thomas carried on his work with Mr Hubber, and he continued to find everything wondrous and fascinating. Occasionally, he went back to Mrs Fishlock's, but he never stayed there for long. Anna was always delighted to see him, but the long absences and his busy life meant that he did not miss her as much as he thought he would.

It was September, and a year since he had left Tunbridge. Thoughts of home and his mama, brothers and sisters infrequently came to his mind. He did, of course, think fondly of Yank, especially as he was constantly reminded of his work, which was going on all around him.

Today, he would be heading back to the now completed tunnel. The entrance looked very grand. First, he needed to settle his rent with his current landlady, a taciturn woman whose manner reminded him of his old tutor, Mr Hargreaves.

"Have you found anywhere to stay yet?" she asked.

"Yes, luckily, I have heard of lodgings near the tunnel. I shall be going there tomorrow."

"I shall… um, I shall miss you."

Thomas's eyes opened wide in surprise. Mrs Morton had always given him the impression that he wasn't welcome. He thought how you could never truly know people.

"You have been very kind to me," he said, thinking how he wouldn't miss his landlady one bit.

After bidding her farewell, he strode along the familiar track from Bletchingley towards Tunbridge. As he walked, nearly everyone he passed acknowledged him in some way by either waving, shouting or patting him, sometimes painfully, on the back.

He'd heard the opening of the line as far as Tunbridge would be in May next year, and he wondered if he might get an invitation to the ceremony. So intently was he dreaming that he failed to hear the wagon on the track behind him, nor someone shouting, "Keep clear." He fell to the ground, twisting his foot as the wagon struck him and hitting his head.

Several men and boys rushed over, and one of

them tugged his foot, which had been caught under a rail. Thomas groaned.

"What'll we do?" the boy asked, staring at the blood coming from the wound to Thomas's head.

"He's Hubber's boy. Go find him," said a man who seemed to have some authority over the group.

The boy scuttled off. Thankfully, Mr Hubber wasn't too far away, and he arrived within half an hour and demanded an explanation. Then he added, "Get someone to fetch a doctor – tell them that it's urgent and he'll be paid."

He turned his attention to Thomas. "Layton, Layton?" he said. There was no response, so Mr Hubber lent over Thomas, whom he had become quite attached to over the last few months. "Can you hear me? Speak to me." The contractor pushed the blood-coated hair from his temple then looked down his body; his ankle seemed to be at an abnormal angle.

There was a slight movement and a sound. He bent his head to catch what he might say. "How hurt are you? Can you say? Are you in pain?"

"Yang," Thomas muttered before drifting from reality. He still hadn't come round by the time the doctor arrived. Mr Hubber explained that the lad appeared to have been struck by a wagon and had hit his head as he fell. Someone had shouted out, but it was too late.

"Is he one of the navvies?"

"No, he works for me."

"What on earth was he doing walking along the line?"

"Lots of men walk along the track. Knowing the boy, he was probably daydreaming."

The doctor examined Thomas and then asked for help to turn him over.

"The gash on his head looks to have concussed him, in which case, he should recover with rest, but in all honesty, I cannot say if his injury is more serious." He looked at Thomas's leg. "I think this might be broken. I'll put a splint on it." The doctor ran his finger around his collar before searching in his bag.

Thomas opened his eyes, coughed and, much to Mr Hubber's and the doctor's disgust, vomited.

"Head aches, want Yang… get Yang."

"Who's he talking about? Who's Yang?" the doctor asked. He was anxious to leave, as he was beginning to feel quite unwell himself.

"No idea. He mentioned that word a while ago," Mr Hubber said. "Maybe it's the name of someone he knows."

The doctor turned back to Thomas, but he had retreated into a coma.

"Well, that's the best I can do for now, but he will need further attention. The bandage will need changing at least and…" He mopped his brow and left quickly, leaving the sentence unfinished.

Mr Hubber wasn't sure where Thomas was lodging, only that prior to coming to the tunnel, he was in Edenbridge. It was obvious a more suitable environment needed to be found for the boy, and soon. Leaving him in the care of one of the navvies, he went back to his hut and looked amongst his papers to see if he had written Thomas's address down, but he couldn't find it anywhere. Frustrated, he poked his head out of his office and called to a lad he thought he could trust. "I want you to go into Edenbridge and try to find out exactly where my runner, Thomas Layton, lives. Do you know who I'm talking about?"

"Yeah, I've seen him."

"He's had an accident and I want to know where he lodged. I don't know the exact address, but it's in Edenbridge. When you've found the house, tell them about the accident." The boy didn't move. "I'll give you thruppence when you return. Go, go now!"

The boy set off, wearily thinking about his near ten-mile round trip.

"Anything to report?" Mr Hubber asked when he returned to check on Thomas.

"No, sir. He's been unconscious since you left."

The contractor had witnessed many injuries while working on the railways, and the men usually dealt with them, clubbing together to pay for a doctor or a pharmacist if they thought the injury was bad enough. Otherwise, the injured person rested for a while and then got back to work if he could. There was an attitude amongst the navvies that you had to appear manly.

Thomas was different. He was extremely well educated and intelligent, but his interest in the railway had brought him to this sorry state. There was a slight movement and Thomas opened his eyes.

"Are you feeling better?" Mr Hubber leaned closer.

"Where am I?"

"On the track near—"

"Track, what track… where?" Thomas didn't wait for an answer. "Get Yank."

"Who's Yank?"

"Bricklayer. Tunbridge." Thomas closed his eyes and said "Anna" before drifting off again.

* * *

It was around midnight when Mr Hubber's boy returned with the news that a Mrs Fishlock was Thomas's landlady, and that she'd agreed for Thomas to be taken there.

Anna, her face streaked with tears, was at the window awaiting his arrival. She'd been inconsolable when her mother had told her that he'd been badly hurt.

"Anna, pull yourself together," she'd said. "You wouldn't want Thomas to see you like this. We must look after him, and having you crying all over him will do him no good."

"What's happened to him?" Anna had asked.

"I'm not sure. The boy who came to tell me the news said he was hit by a wagon on a railway line, and that his leg was broken and his head was bleeding."

"Here he is!" Anna shouted now from her position at the window. She rushed out into the road, ignoring her mother's plea to stay where she was. Hitching up her skirt, she climbed into the wagon. "Thomas, oh, Thomas, what have you done?"

He was in no state to reply. The waggoner said that to the best of his knowledge, the lad had been unconscious for most of the journey. With his help, Mrs Fishlock carried him into the house and laid him on the canvas bed that she'd made up for him near the fire.

"Has he been seen by anyone?" she enquired.

"I was told a doctor had looked over him. Mr Hubber paid for it."

"Of course, I remember the name now. How bad are his injuries?"

"I'm sorry, I've no idea. I was asked to bring him here because I'm on my way back to Tunbridge. I expect Mr Hubber will come and see you… erm, sometime."

Privately, the waggoner thought this unlikely. There was nothing special about this accident. In his experience, they happened all the time.

While his mother was chatting to the waggoner, Anna knelt beside Thomas and tried to get him to speak.

"Anna, he cannot talk to you, he's too badly injured. We'll get Dr Evans to see to him. Run along to his house and explain the situation as best you can."

"But I don't want to leave him, Mama."

Mrs Fishlock was standing by the range stirring a pot. "No, I'm sure you don't, but I have to see to this meal. You'll only be gone a few minutes. He won't come to any harm in that short time, will he?"

She was doing her best to reassure her daughter, but she was doubtful that Thomas would recover. Such serious head injuries were nearly always fatal.

Anna flew to the doctor's house and gabbled her requirements. He knew her well, having been present at her birth, and told her to explain things more slowly. When she had finished speaking, he realised the importance of a home visit.

"Can you come now, Dr Evans? He won't talk to me. I think he's going to die." She started to sob, and the doctor agreed to come straight away.

"Anna tells me that this young man has been unconscious throughout his journey here," he said to Mrs Fishlock when they arrived at the house. "Have you any idea how long ago he was wounded? He has a nasty gash on his head, which looks as if it has been cleaned."

"All my information has come in bits and pieces passed on from different people," Mrs Fishlock replied. "A doctor has seen him, but I think Thomas is drifting in and out of consciousness. He hasn't spoken all the time he's been here, about twenty or thirty minutes, but the waggoner who brought him said that a contractor told him he has spoken a few words and mentioned someone called Yank."

"He's told me about Yank!" Anna said eagerly. "Thomas used to know him when he was living in Leigh."

Dr Evans examined Thomas to see if there were any injuries other than the ones he had been told about. He lifted his eyelids and peered into his eyes, then he lifted each of his arms. "This wound," he said, pointing to the gash on his head, "that's where something hit him?"

"Yes," Mrs Fishlock replied. "The boy who brought the message yesterday said he'd been hit by a wagon, but I don't think the wagon did it. He possibly hit something on the ground."

Dr Evans looked surprised. "Why wasn't the lad warned?" he asked, returning to his inspection of Thomas's body. "Has he been sick?"

"I don't know."

Reaching the same conclusion as the first doctor,

Dr Evans said, "At best he has been concussed, at worst, I think he has fractured his skull. He needs careful treatment if that's the case, and his leg could be fractured or broken." The doctor tried to move his leg, but Thomas moaned. "You say someone qualified attended to him at the time?"

"Yes, the contractor got a doctor."

"Well, his bandage needs changing." He peered at Thomas's left leg again and then raised it. "Hmmm, could just be his ankle that's broken."

All the while, Thomas stirred but did not wake.

"Hey, Big Yank, Boss wants to see you. You're needed in Edenbridge."

"In Edenbridge? But I was there about eighteen months ago, before I was sent to Leigh. Why would I be wanted back there? There's enough work here in Tunbridge."

"You're to go to a Mrs Fishlock's house," Yank's boss told him. "Someone, a boy I believe, is seriously injured and calls for you. I wasn't given an address – just Edenbridge."

Yank knew at once that it was Thomas. "Who sent for me?"

"Mr Hubber, the contractor. He sent a message asking that you be relieved of your duties for a while."

No matter how they were caused, neither

engineers nor contractors were in the business of tending to injuries on the railway.

Yank was overcome. "How bad is he?" he asked.

"I'm told he's not expected to live. I'll release you without pay, but I expect you to be back here as quickly as possible."

Yank's heart sank at this news, and he quickly turned away so he could not be seen trying to hold back his tears.

Chapter Seventeen

YANK TRIED to hitch a lift on a wagon carrying railway equipment, but unfortunately, there was nothing available, so he stopped at The Chequers to purchase a flagon of ale and then stocked up on some food from Saunders, the grocers near the Bull Inn. His intention was to follow the road as the wagons would do, and maybe get a lift that way. But whilst waiting for his order to be wrapped, he had second thoughts about the journey and guessed his best and quickest plan would be to follow the permanent way; this would be the most direct route on foot. The railway was being fenced along its route, but no one would bother him, especially as many of the railway workers knew him by sight. He would go onto the road whenever his path was blocked by ongoing works.

Yank reckoned it was about three miles to Leigh, and once there he took a detour to tell Mrs Grimley about Thomas. She had taken such a shine to him that he felt she ought to know. She greeted Yank like a long-lost son and was distressed to hear about Thomas. She made Yank promise he would let her know what happened to him.

He returned to the track at Leigh, climbing the embankment and crossing the bridge over the road. After another mile and a half, he reached Penshurst Station. He had been walking for more than two hours by now, so he stopped to rest and eat. He estimated a good few miles still lay ahead.

When he reached Edenbridge, he searched for the Albion Hotel. He had been told that Thomas's landlady, Mrs Fishlock, lived nearby. After making a few enquiries he knocked on the Fishlocks' door, which was promptly opened by a pretty young girl.

"I'm Yank. I've—"

His hand was grabbed, and he was pulled into the hall. "He's been asking for you. He's in here." She hauled him into the kitchen, where he found Mrs Fishlock sitting on a chair beside Thomas.

She stood up as he approached. "Yours is the only name he mentions when he rouses. Our doctor thinks he has a fractured skull, and even with expert treatment he—"

Anna let out a heartrending cry and put her hand to her mouth.

Yank squatted beside the makeshift bed. "I've come, Thomas, just as you asked." He took the still delicate white hand in his rough one. There was no response when Yank squeezed it.

"Thomas, Thomas, listen to me. Remember when we were at Mrs Grimley's and her awful meals? You didn't like them, did you? But you wouldn't upset her by saying so."

"I am afraid he is too far gone," Mrs Fishlock commented, close to tears herself. "He needs to be in a hospital or treated by the best doctors, but I expect even then he will not recover." Very quietly, Yank heard her add, "I have become so very fond of him."

Yank was of the same opinion, but he wasn't going to leave without fighting for his friend.

"I think, Mrs Fishlock, that he ought to go back to his own home."

"But... but he told us he was an orphan, from London," she said. "Though I did have my suspicions all was not quite as it seemed."

"He comes from a good home in the north of Tunbridge, but he ran away."

He did not want to burden them with the details. "I met him in Leigh, and my landlady and I sheltered him. Then he ran away again."

As he spoke, he again wondered if he was to blame for that.

There was a slight movement from Thomas and his hand moved in Yank's. The bricklayer bent to catch his words as Anna rushed over.

"Yank... heard you... help me."

"I think you ought to go home where you can be looked after by your own doctor. He will know what to do."

"Did you say home? I can't hear… my father."

"Your father will not harm you, but I haven't the money to pay for the care you need. It'll be for the best, and I promise you that no one… no one will ever treat you like you were treated before. Do you believe me, Thomas?"

Thomas nodded and closed his eyes.

"Have you a carrier nearby who could take him to Tunbridge, ma'am?"

"Jonas will take him," said Anna, leaping up and rushing from the kitchen before she could be stopped. "I'll get him."

"I'm afraid my daughter will not rest until Thomas is seen to. I only hope we are not too late. She is distraught as it is and will make herself ill. I don't know what else can be done if Jonas isn't available. All the carriers seem to be working for the railway. It's more profitable, of course."

Yank nodded. "The work's easing up a bit now, but—"

Anna flew into the kitchen, fanning the flames of the range as she did so. "I met him in the road," she said. "He says he will come now and asked what payment he would receive."

"I'll pay him," Yank said, trusting he was not going to have to haggle at such a crucial and upsetting time.

"I can help," Mrs Fishlock said, taking her purse from the mantelpiece. Anna added that she was looking after some money for Thomas.

The carrier suggested one and sixpence, which Yank and Anna's mother considered acceptable, as he had to compete with the railway's demands.

"I wonder if you would help me take Thomas to your wagon?" Yank asked Jonas. "It would be best to leave him on this bed. The less we move him the better." Yank had seen many a railway man with injuries that might have been better mended had they not been hauled roughly by the arms and legs with no other support.

"I will go with Thomas," he said, glancing at Jonas to see if this was acceptable. Then he turned to Mrs Fishlock. "And I will try and get a message to you on how well he is."

By seven that evening, the party arrived at Mr Laird's front door. It was opened by the housemaid.

"I would like to speak to Mr Laird, please. My name is Big Yank, and Mr Laird will know who I am." Then Yank added, "I would also like Mrs Laird and her eldest daughter to be told of my arrival."

The housemaid stared at Yank as she contemplated this unusual request. "Hurry. I have Tobias outside and he is seriously ill."

She knocked on the nearby door and Yank could hear her explaining his message.

Mr Laird appeared from a room to the left of the front door. He was closely followed by Mrs Laird. The housemaid disappeared, and Yank hoped it was to fetch the sister.

"What have we here and who are you?" Mr Laird boomed, obviously not recognising Yank, or else choosing not to.

"I have brought your son. He is at death's door, and he should be treated by a doctor – a good doctor – immediately. If I had the money, I would pay for it."

Mrs Laird pushed past her husband and Yank to go to the wagon she could see at the gate. Yank followed, and with Jonas's help, they took Thomas, who was still on the makeshift bed, into the house.

Mr Laird went to speak.

"I'll deal with this, Septimus," said Amelia, "you have done enough." She turned to the men. "Take him upstairs."

When she looked up, she saw her younger children peering over the banisters. Lizzie was coming down the stairs, followed by the housemaid.

"Elizabeth, show these gentlemen where Tobias's room is."

The servants had gathered in the hall. The entire household now knew of Tobias's return, and they whispered to each other and gasped when he was taken upstairs. They stared at Mr Laird as he tried and failed to get a grip on the situation before disappearing into his study and loudly shutting the door.

In the bedroom, Yank explained the situation to Mrs Laird as best he could, and she sent Lizzie to tell Dawkins to saddle Ember and fetch Dr Vincent.

"The injury to your son was the day before yesterday, ma'am. By all accounts, he was hit by a wagon. I was told it happened as he walked along the track. I don't know where exactly." He took a deep breath. "I fear it—"

"Yes, I understand. You have been most kind. Do we owe you any money?"

"No, ma'am."

With careful instruction from Yank, Tobias was lifted onto his own bed. This movement appeared to rouse him. "Yank, are you there? Head aches... where am I?"

"I have brought you home. Your mother and sister are here beside me."

Tobias opened his eyes and murmured "Mama" before closing them again.

"Tobias, dearest. We have missed you so much."

But Tobias was no longer listening.

Lizzie drew closer to the bed; she was too upset to say anything. Yank glanced at her and saw how intelligent she appeared and how much Thomas, or should he say Tobias, meant to her. Her eyes were brimming with tears that glistened in the candlelight as she tried to keep her emotions in check.

Yank was doing the same. "I guess I ought to go now, Mrs Laird—"

"No, no, I will not hear of it. You must stay here overnight. You will wish to hear what the doctor says, will you not? Besides, Tobias may ask for you again."

"Yes, Mrs Laird, ma'am, but I don't want to cause you any trouble. I guess you have enough to deal with, and my clothes are not..." He indicated his appearance with a sweep of his hand. "And I must return to work."

Mrs Laird ignored his plea and her second son, James, who'd joined the sorry scene, was instructed to get the housemaid to make up the bed in the spare room and prepare a bath to be put in the room so their guest could wash that evening. An hour later, the doctor arrived, and Mr Laird eventually emerged from his study.

"I hear, Laird, that your son has returned, and not in good circumstances." The doctor's voice was censorious. He had always suspected there was more to Tobias's disappearance than met the eye. Rumours had abounded for some time. A boy does not leave a good home unless he has been ill-treated, and he knew that Laird had a violent temper. The groom, he had gathered, did not think much of his master, either.

"I'll come upstairs with you," Mr Laird said,

though in reality, he did not want to see Tobias, his injuries, or the American his wife had invited to stay the night without first asking his permission.

"No," the doctor said, firmly. "I need to deal with this. Your wife is upstairs, I assume?"

Though the doctor admitted to himself he did not have much evidence, he suspected Laird had probably caused all this in the first place.

Meanwhile, Laird was pleased on the one hand and affronted on the other. Who was this man to tell him whether he could or could not see his own son?

Yank relayed to Dr Vincent all the details he'd been told about the accident. As the events had been relayed several times and passed on by different people, the American was none too certain if even Thomas knew exactly what had happened to him. Was it a wagon that had hit him? Surely Thomas would know what was coming along a track. He must have walked along them hundreds of times. How bad was the gash on his head, and was it from the wagon or a fall? And how badly was his leg broken, or was it his ankle? Whatever had occurred, his prospects weren't good if it was his skull that had been damaged.

"You say the doctor in Edenbridge tended to his leg?"

"I'm not sure. I mean, I'm not sure who saw him immediately after the accident. Whoever did might not have been a doctor – more likely a pharmacist.

Railway workers tend not to call out doctors, as pharmacists are cheaper, that is if they get them any help at all."

Dr Vincent inspected the crude splint. "Hmmm, not bad, but he'll probably have a permanent limp. I think his ankle might have twisted when he fell."

"I was told his leg was broken," said Yank.

The doctor studied Thomas's head wound, which was relatively clean and had been covered with a bandage that he concluded must have been changed since the accident. "Has he vomited?"

Yank shrugged. "I don't know."

"You say he drifts in and out of consciousness?"

"Yes, we gathered that from Mr Hubber and Mrs Fishlock."

"Who's Mr Hubber?"

"He's the contractor that Thom… Tobias has been working for on the railway."

"He's been working on the railway!" Mrs Laird exclaimed.

"Yes, ever since I met him, he has been keen to do that, but he was not strong enough to do the physical work."

"So, what was he doing?" Lizzie asked.

"When he had the accident, I understand he was a runner, that is, he took messages from and to Mr Hubber."

While Dr Vincent was inspecting Tobias's head

and the whole of his body, Elizabeth was sent from the room.

The doctor looked up at Yank. "Can you help me? I want to see if there is any damage to his back."

With Yank on one side and the doctor and Mrs Laird on the other, they turned Tobias onto his side and pulled up his shirt. Yank waited to see their reaction.

"What's this?" the doctor exclaimed. "It looks as if he's been assaulted. The scars have healed well but they must have been deep. Would he have been in some sort of fight?" He glanced up at Yank.

"Those aren't the results of a fight, sir."

"How do you know? You can't see them from there."

"I met him the day after they were… were done."

Yank glanced at Mrs Laird and their eyes met. He could see she knew exactly what had occurred.

"I think we might put some leeches around the head wound. Let us hope the fracture has not broken the bones of the scalp, which will have caused damage to the brain. I'm afraid, Mrs Laird, there is nothing more I can suggest. It's just a matter of time to see if he recovers." He saw her distress. "I'm sure he will. He's a strong lad, and he has been well fed and looked after."

"What can we do, Mama?" Elizabeth asked, on re-entering the bedroom. She was anxious to be part of any healing process her dear brother might need.

"Keep him warm," the doctor replied. "Make him drink some cordial when he rouses, and talk to him, even if you think he cannot hear you. I will change the bandage when I return tomorrow. The wound is clean and seems to be healing well. All we can do now is pray that his brain has not been affected. Only time will tell."

* * *

Tobias was in a room of staggering, bright white light; there were no windows in this room, but he could see figures: a woman with her arm round a girl in a fur hat, an older woman in a cape carrying a baby. He could hear his mother's voice, but he could not see her. Then the light dimmed a little and there was Yank – dear, dear Yank. He held out his arms and the American took hold of him. He had been in a very dark place, but now he felt safe.

He opened his eyes. "Yank, oh, Yank. You came to me just as I asked."

"Mrs Laird," Yank called. He turned to Tobias. "You've come round at last."

"Where am I?"

"Don't you remember?"

Yank felt a movement beside him. "Here is your mother."

"Tobias, my darling. Can you hear me?"

"Yes, Mama, and I can see you." He glanced around his bedroom. "Have I been home long?"

"You came yesterday. Your friend brought you from Edenbridge."

There was a knock on the bedroom door and Elizabeth rushed in. "Tobias, are you well now? Do you feel better? Can you sit up? The others want to see you."

"I sure think we ought to take things easy," Yank said. "We must wait for the doctor and listen to what he says. I guess he won't want to rush things. He was in a very serious way, you know."

"Come, Elizabeth. We shall go and tell the children and your father that Tobias is recovering."

"But I want to stay with him, Mama."

"Yes, I know, but we must not tire him. Let his friend here explain what has happened and perhaps later all of us can come and speak to him." She smiled. "One at a time, I think, would be appropriate."

"Yes, Mama, very well."

Chapter Eighteen

For the next few days, Tobias wasn't allowed to leave his bedroom, even though he assured Doctor Vincent that he was now well. All his siblings visited him, including baby Charlotte, who was brought to him by the nursemaid. Tobias exclaimed how much she had grown since he last saw her, and he was informed that the child was now walking. The nurse put her on the floor to show him.

Elizabeth was at his bedside at every opportunity, even when she'd been told not to by her mother. Yank stayed the first night, as requested by Mrs Laird, but the next morning he had to impress upon her the necessity to return to work. Mrs Laird seemed surprised at this but thanked him profusely for all he had done for her son. She said he was to return to see Tobias as often as he wished.

His father came to visit Tobias soon after. He

stood at the foot of his bed before moving to sit on James's. "Um... your mother says you have, um, you have... you're better now."

"Yes, Father, I am much better."

"Good, that's good." He put his hands on his thighs and slid them up and down. "Doctor Vincent says you must stay in bed for a few more days."

'Yes, Father, I know. I wanted to get up, but he said to wait a little longer."

"Quite so, quite so." His father sat silently for what seemed to Tobias an eternity.

"Father," Tobias said eventually. "I would like to go to school. I want to go to university and study to be an engineer."

His father raised his eyebrows. When Mr Laird decided that all his children should be educated at home, it was because he wished to have control over what they were taught. Matters would be out of his hands if Tobias, or any of his children, went away to be schooled. University wasn't something he had ever considered.

"Well, do you approve?"

"I must think about it. It will involve some expense."

"Yes, of course. I hadn't thought clearly." He looked over at his father. "But I do want to be an engineer, and I want to have something to do with the railways. Perhaps I could be apprenticed."

"Apprenticed!" his father said, appalled. "But that's for—"

"Yes, I know, Papa... poor people." Tobias marvelled over the way he was speaking to his father. "I just thought how it wouldn't involve so much money."

His father stood up, reached for the gold watch in his pocket, coughed and said he must go.

"You will think about it, won't you?" Tobias said, as his father reached the door.

Tobias felt he had a hold over his father because of the beating, and because his mother was now asserting herself. She was only seventeen when she married, and his father was considerably older. With no experience of the world and being of a quiet nature, she had become used to having any opinion she held dismissed by her husband till she no longer had any thoughts of her own. How pleasant it was now to see his mama come to life. He would not treat his own wife like that.

Thoughts of having a wife recalled Anna to his mind. How was she? Did she know he was ill? Where did Yank say he had found him? He rang the bell beside his bed and his sister came into the room almost immediately.

"Good heavens, Lizzie, were you standing outside the door?"

"No, but I was close by. I was coming to see you before I go to lessons."

"Oh." He had forgotten all about his tutor. What would he think about him going to school? "How is old Hargreaves?"

"As miserable as ever. We are studying Shakespeare now. *The Merchant of Venice*." His sister touched Tobias's hand. "I have missed you so much." She remembered the bell tinkling. "Did you want something?"

"I've forgotten how I got here and where I came from. I can't remember if Yank told me or not." He paused. "Was Mr Hubber angry with me?"

"I don't know who Mr Hubber is, and I didn't speak to Yank. He looked a bit rough."

"Yank is a marvellous man," Tobias said defensively. "I don't care what he looks like. He was wonderfully kind to me."

"All right, all right, don't get upset or I shall get the blame. You had better calm down. Mama says you can get up tomorrow. Are you in any pain?"

"My ankle hurts. I have only stood on it a few times since I came round. Doctor Vincent says I will have a limp, as the bones haven't set properly."

Their mother came into the room, her gown swaying as she approached the bed. Tobias thought how pretty and elegant she looked. He'd never studied his mother closely before. She seemed younger than when he'd left home.

"I thought I heard the bell."

"Yes, Mama, I heard it too. Tobias wants to know where Yank found him."

"You were taken to where you were staying, a Mrs Fishlock's, I believe, in Edenbridge."

"Ah, yes, and Anna? Do you know about Anna?"

"Who's Anna?" Lizzie asked, feeling a slight moment of disquiet.

"She's Mrs Fishlock's daughter. We used to go walking together. She's very nice. You'll like her, Lizzie."

His sister was thinking otherwise.

"Your friend might come this evening: you can ask him to make everything clearer. It's obvious you are not fully recovered from your ordeal. Your wounds, perhaps, but not your mind. Come, Elizabeth, we must not tire him."

* * *

It was two evenings later when Yank arrived back at the house, and he was greeted by Mrs Laird as if he were a relative. He found Tobias sitting on a chair by his bed.

"Look, Yank, I have been walking round the room. Watch me."

Tobias stood up and walked towards him. It was obvious that he was in some pain when his foot touched the floor, but he was so proud of himself.

"That's wonderful, Thomas, I mean, Tobias." He

grinned. "How are you? I would have come sooner, but we have been so busy, and I have not been finishing till late, so by the time I had walked here, you would have all been asleep."

Tobias was now close to Yank, and he threw his arms around him. "I have missed you so much," he said. "I wanted to tell you all about how I was able to work for the railway, despite what you said, *and* I have asked my father if I can go to school and university to study to be an engineer."

Tears ran down his cheeks as he searched Yank's face for his approval.

"Goodness, then you'll become my chief."

"And I shall send you all over Kent, so you won't know where you are."

They laughed.

Yank felt close to tears as he studied Tobias's face, which was radiant as he talked of his future, though almost twelve months of hard toil showed in the maturity of his features. "Sit down, Tobias," he said gently. "You mustn't do too much at a time."

Tobias fell into a chair with a big sigh. "I can't remember all you said about bringing me back here," he admitted.

Yank told him how he'd been hit by a wagon, and how he'd twisted his ankle, which was thought to be broken at first, and sustained a head injury. Yank reckoned he got this when he hit the ground.

"You were not expected to live, and to tell you the

truth, Thom… Tobias, I heard so many different versions of the accident, from all sorts of people, that I couldn't work out what was the truth.

"They found out where you lodged in Edenbridge, but don't ask me how, cause I don't know."

Seeing Tobias was about to open his mouth again, Yank continued. "Your landlady said you could be brought to her, and a doctor saw you there. You kept asking for me."

"Did I? I don't remember. I don't remember much at all."

Just as well, Yank thought.

"Then what happened?"

"You called me Yang at first, and nobody knew what it meant. But Anna knew about me, and a message was sent to me. Speaking of Anna, you had a lovely young lady very upset about you." Yank winked at him and a flush crossed Tobias's face.

"Because I knew where you lived, I suggested that you were brought home. So, here you are. I'm sure I did tell you some of this, you know."

"Sorry." Tobias grinned. A vague memory of someone tugging his leg popped into his head.

"Never mind," Yank replied. "You'll soon be back to your usual self. Now, why don't you tell me why you ran away from Mrs Grimley's? I must report back to her. She was very upset when you left, and even more upset when I told her about your accident."

* * *

Lizzie came into Tobias's bedroom. "A Mrs Fishlock and her daughter are here to see you. Are you well enough?"

Tobias was sitting in his chair reading *The Merchant of Venice,* which Mr Hargreaves said he had to finish before he returned to his daily studies.

"Oh, how lovely, does Mama know? Go and tell her and then they can come and see me."

Lizzie was not enamoured with the visitors, especially when Anna rushed over to her brother and kissed his cheek.

"Thomas, I've missed you so, and I thought you were going to die. Are you better? Yes, of course you are."

Mrs Fishlock took hold of her daughter's arm. "Anna, do not be so familiar. Mrs Laird does not want her son getting too excited, and you are a guest here, remember."

Anna looked contrite. Mrs Laird told her to sit on one of the beds while she and Tobias recounted what had happened to him after he had left the Fishlock residence.

Lizzie, who had heard it all before, could not wait for this girl, pretty though she had to admit she was, to be gone. She sat glowering as far away from her as she could.

Anna and her mother were engrossed by what had transpired.

"Are you going to go back on the railway, Thomas?" Anna asked hopefully, thinking he might return and stay in Edenbridge.

"No, my father says I can go to school, then university, so I can become an engineer on the railway. There will be lots of work for me when I've qualified," Tobias explained, confident all would go just as he planned.

"Oh, I'll never see you ever again." Anna began to cry.

Mrs Fishlock, realising that it was time to go, stood up and took her leave of Mrs Laird and her daughter. She could sense she would have a miserable, moody young girl moping over the loss of her one and only true love for at least another month. Thomas didn't know what to say, so he just smiled at Anna. Their walks together seemed so long ago.

Epilogue

FOLLOWING HIS RECOVERY, Tobias took life, or was forced to take life, extremely carefully. He read everything he could about what was happening in and around Tunbridge and further towards Dover.

Now the great day had arrived, and the line to Tunbridge from Red Hill was to be celebrated on 24 May 1842. Mr Hubber remembered him and made sure he was invited to the ceremony. Though not among the important guests, he was nevertheless shown to an area where he could see everything that was taking place. Tobias decided this was the happiest day of his life, but he was disappointed to see that not many of the navvies were present to have their hard work acknowledged.

Mr Laird did allow Tobias go to school and university. Though the patriarch continued to be pompous and bossy, he mellowed with the subtle support of Amelia, and the household became a more pleasant place in which to live and work.

Tobias completed his studies and did, as he always hoped, become a railway engineer. He was renowned for his compassion towards those less fortunate than himself.

Not to be outdone, Lizzie was also allowed to go to school and she went on to become a teacher. This was as far as she was able to go within the constraints of her gender. James, less ambitious than his older siblings, went into accounting. The younger son, Joseph, emigrated to Australia, whilst the girls married and lived in the area.

Charlotte, however, was the brightest of them all and became one of the first women to study medicine.

Anna lost touch with Thomas, but after a few weeks of tearful reminiscences, she found other young admirers.

Yank, quite content with being a bricklayer, stayed in Kent and eventually started a small company of his own. He married a Kentish girl, and they had five children. He, Tobias and Mrs Grimley kept in sporadic contact.

Bibliography

The Railway Navvies, by Terry Chapman, 1968

John Stevens, Leigh Historical Society, 2013

The Railway Navvy, by David Brooke, 1983

The Illustrated Guide to the South Eastern Railway, by George Measom, 1853

The Pictorial Times, c 1842, page showing drawings of Bletchingley Tunnel

Maidstone Journal

Prevention, Detection and Keepers of the Peace, by Pam Mills, 2022

Acknowledgments

I would like to thank John Smallman Smith for reading my first draft and Pam Mills for her assistance with the workings of the constabulary in the 1840s.

Finally, a big thank you to Danielle from Wrate's Editing Services for her help with the editing and production of my novel, and to her team, Abby, who did the proofreading, and Rachel, who designed the cover.

About the Author

Marie was born in Clapham, London, and has always been an avid reader. After O-levels and a secretarial course, she started work as a shorthand typist in the City.

Marie married in 1957 and moved to Tonbridge in

1961. She took exams to become a typewriting teacher and stayed in teaching after taking an Open University degree in the '80s. She did not start writing until she retired, and her first three novels were self-published.